WASPS AT THE SPEED OF SOUND

WASPS AT THE SPEED OF SOUND

DERRYL MURPHY

PRIME BOOKS

PUBLICATION HISTORY
"Lost Jenny" originally appeared in *On Spec,* Fall 1999.
"Island of the Moon" originally appeared in *Neo-opsis,* Fall 2003.
"Those Graves of Memory" originally appeared in *Future Orbits,* February 2002.
"Father Time" originally appeared in *Tesseracts 4,* ed. by Michael Skeet and Lorna Toolis, 1992.
"Day's Hunt" originally appeared in *TransVersions 5,* Spring 1996.
"Wasps at the Speed of Sound" originally appeared in *Oceans of the Mind,* Winter 2002.
"What Goes Around" originally appeared in *Tesseracts 6,* ed. by Robert J. Sawyer and Carolyn Clink, 1997.
"Blue Train" originally appeared in *land/space,* ed. by Candas Jane Dorsey and Judy McCroskey, 2002.
"The Abbey Engine" originally appeared in *Oceans of the Mind,* March 2002.
"The History of Photography" originally appeared in *Prairie Fire,* Fall 1994.
"Summer's Humans" is original to this volume.

Prime Books
www.prime-books.com

CONTENTS

For George and Nadine Murphy—
parents, allies, and sometimes even critics

INTRODUCTION

A few years ago, Derryl Murphy and I were hiking around a cottage-infested lake somewhere in central Alberta. While we hashed over topics ranging from cloned Christs to ex-girlfriends, the part of our conversation that most virally stuck in my mind was Murph's proposition that spiders are better at mathematics than insects because they have more legs to count on. This is what allows them to build interdimensional portals into their webs.

The *artiste* in me had about ten seconds to revel in the mind-blowing beauty of this idea before my anal-rententive scientist persona squashed it flat. "How do they *do* it?" I wanted to know. "Why didn't they do it before? Is it brains, or some hardwired instinct that only kicks in under extreme stress? And how come—"

Derryl's reply—I'm paraphrasing here—was "Watts, who gives a shit? It's a *story.*"

He was right, of course. It was a story—and a pretty good one to boot—but more fundamentally, he was right to realize that cool ideas and narrative drive matter more in this game than do technical specs. That frees Derryl as a writer, in a way that I can only envy.

Plunk us both down in the same imaginary world and he'll be wandering its outback like a native while I'm still standing in the bus station, face scrunched up over the tourist map, trying to make sense of the grid references.

I, you see, was trained as a scientist, and I write what's commonly called "hard science fiction," but I think Derryl knows something about that particular brand of storytelling that I've only recently allowed myself to admit: it doesn't actually *exist,* in any objective sense. The "hardness" of fictional science does not reflect the author's rigor so much as the reader's credulity. I can—I *have*—spent days poring over scientific journals to figure out how some fictitious apocalyptic microbe might avoid lysis once it penetrates the host cell; a real microbiologist would still regard my solution as pure fantasy, while the average reader might end up more bored than enlightened by the technospeak. Too much expertise can be a straitjacket; too slavish a devotion to *science* turns *fiction* into crap.

Derryl knows this. And so he can reinvent *Moby Dick* in a landfill site, and soar; and if he leaves the likes of me wondering how his far-future whales got their fingers back, that's really my problem, isn't it? He's too good a writer to muck up a perfectly good story with superfluous nuts and bolts.

Lest some of you think that I'm damning with faint praise here—*Murphy's a great writer because he doesn't care enough to get his facts straight*—let me hasten to point out that the man knows *exactly* how to be rigorous when the situation calls for it. You cannot read a story like "Island of the Moon" without knowing that here is a man who has done his research. (Not many non-biologists would even be able to tell you who Robert MacArthur *is,* much less write a story that cites his work on island biogeography.) And Murphy's real-world expertise with the camera is on plain display in "The History of Photography," which remains (for me at any rate) his signature piece: a little gem which isn't even science fiction, and yet is; in which nothing moves, and yet everything happens. The man is careless with neither his facts nor his conjectures; he simply knows how to keep each in their place.

There's at least one thing that Derryl's fiction and mine have in common, though: a grim, realist view of the future. Whether the world dies of thirst, or nano-goo, or sheer indundation beneath the weight of its own garbage, it will be Human Ingenuity that ultimately pushes the planet over the brink. This may not be a pleasant proposition, or a popular one—your average Mundane would be hard-pressed to dismiss it with the "mindless escapism" label that so frequently hangs around the genre's neck—but the message is more important than ever before. And so may I present to you one Derryl Murphy, another voice in the wilderness, showing us where we're headed in the faint but vital hope that you may yet prove him wrong. And if his stories aren't entirely devoid of hope—if his protagonists manage to turn the tide every now and then, knock down the occasional dam, bring water back to some parched corner of the earth—well, that's just Derryl's inner optimist showing through. And it's his problem, isn't it?

There are a million ways for the planet to die. Derryl Murphy figures you can only handle eleven of them at once. Here they are.

Peter Watts

Peter Watts is a marginally-successful hybrid of marine biologist and science fiction author. He has authored the faintly-acclaimed "Rifters trilogy" *(Starfish, Maelstrom,* and the final volume, split into two, *βehemoth: β-Max* and *βehemoth: Seppuku,* all from Tor), as well as a plethora of shorter tales including the classic *Models of heat loss by marine mammals: thermoregulation below the "Zone of Irrelevance"* and *A comparison of age determination techniques for the harbour porpoise, Phocoena phocoena L.* His short fiction has been collected into an overpriced pamphlet from Tesseract Books *(Ten Monkeys, Ten Minutes),* and has also appeared in venues ranging from *On Spec* to the *Journal of Theoretical Ecology.* His fondness for domestic shorthair cats borders on pathology.

I'm probably setting myself up for some remarks about the Painfully Obvious, but some of my stories have come to me in visions or dreams. This is one of them; an image of some slackers sitting on the side of a hill and taking part in a giant ceilidh, which of course is an image that never made it into the final story. And no, I have no idea how one leads to the other. I've never asked around, but I imagine other writers sometimes experience similar moments, asleep or awake, where seeing or feeling one thing quickly leads to something that seems completely unrelated.

LOST JENNY

Mark sat on the roof of his brother's apartment building, watching as tens of thousands of people filed out of the city by car, by bus, by bike and by foot. From this vantage point overlooking the river valley he could see people making the choice to go north, east and west, and if he got up and walked to the other side of the roof he could see another long line going south. Noises drifted up to him, sounds of panic and fear and anger, sometimes the odd fight breaking out among those almost directly below him, usually between a slow-moving motorist and a pedestrian or biker.

He heard the door to the roof open and close behind him, and leaned back in the lawn chair to see his brother Dave come walking across the gravel, backpack hanging loose over one shoulder. Dave dropped the pack on the roof beside Mark and sat on it, gazed out and watched the crowds for a moment, not saying anything.

"I wish you'd come with us," he finally said, looking up at the roiling storm clouds. Distant thunder crashed, and the wind occasionally gusted across the rooftop, loose gravel and garbage skittering over their feet.

Mark fished a smoke from his pocket, lit it during a brief lull. "To where?" He snorted after inhaling. "No fucking way we're going to escape this. I may as well hang, see if any of my friends are still around, enjoy the last few days."

"But Mom and Dad . . . "

"Fuck Mom and Dad. They kicked me out because they didn't want me around, didn't like what I was." Mark stood up, walked over to the edge and spit. "I appreciate the help you've been for me, big brother, but you and me can say our good-byes right now. Me and the folks said it two years ago." He put a hand on Dave's shoulder, squeezed for a second, then let go and sat back.

Dave sat in silence for a few more seconds, then reached out and took his brother's hand, held it and smiled as he looked at him. Mark smiled back, gave his hand a squeeze in return, then let go. "You gotta move, man. Not much time left to get out of the city."

Dave stood, shouldered his pack. "If we somehow make it through this, I'm coming back, Mark. You keep good care of my apartment."

Mark laughed. "Shit, Dave, nobody gonna make it through this. But I promise you, I'll only trash all the other apartments in the building. Yours stays safe."

"And don't get shot by some asshole who knows you aren't supposed to be here. Keep out of sight."

Mark nodded, waved his hand, then leaned forward to watch the crowds again, not wanting to look his brother in the eye anymore. "Later."

After Dave had left, Mark leaned over the edge and watched until he saw him come out the front door and join the stream of people walking towards oblivion. Then he leaned back and looked at the black and gray sky, and wondered what surprises it and the night would bring.

The radio still worked, the people at CBC One doing a decent job of keeping everyone up to date. For a while there, CNN and Newsworld had been coming in loud and clear as well, but the cable company had crapped out a couple of days before, and in this building the reception without an antenna was for shit, not even worth checking for non-cable stations. Mark lay in bed, listening to the radio and to the background noise of people still trying to escape the city, sad quiet moments of music punctuated by the latest breathless news report of the continuing destruction.

California to at least the edge of the Sierra Nevadas was gone, said a reporter, apparently doing a live report from near the top of some peak, wind roaring past the mike as he shouted to be heard. It was amazing the satellites still worked, but Mark had heard earlier that the aliens still wanted some communications while they continued their search and demands; no one knew how they were able to control the destruction so precisely. The Pacific Ocean had rushed in to fill the gap when coastal California and part of the continental shelf beyond had disappeared, said the reporter, describing waves smashing against stark cliffs that towered hundreds and sometimes thousands of feet above the water, marching in an unerringly even line as far north and south as the borders of Oregon and Mexico. Tens of millions had vanished in this latest event—they were *events* now, not tragedies—alive one second, removed from any form of existence the next.

The next report concerned the fugitive alien, still on the loose despite demands she turn herself in. People around the world were panicking, and in some countries women were being slaughtered wholesale in the misplaced belief that one of them would be the missing alien, and that presenting her body to the rest of her kind floating in space somewhere past what was left of the Moon would somehow stem the tide of destruction and even change its course.

Third, Mark listened to updates and analysis about the alien demands for people to clear out of all cities with populations over fifty thousand. One commentator felt that this was evidence that the alien they were seeking was somehow restricted to a city, and that they would be better able to search her out without all the millions of other bodies in the way. Made sense to Mark. Maybe they'd already ruled out all of the big cities in California.

Finally, Mark thumbed the remote, shut off the radio. He closed his eyes and tried to sleep, but after almost an hour of listening to the people on the streets below and not being able to doze off, he got up, got dressed and grabbed a couple of beers, turned the big stereo on and cranked up a Buffalo Tom CD, and went to the asshole neighbor's apartment across the hall. No answer when he knocked, not that he expected one, so several good hard kicks with his boot and he was in. For the next two hours he slowly sipped at his Warthogs and methodically trashed the place, ripping pictures from the walls and flinging them like Frisbees across the room, bashing in faucets, smashing plates and glasses on the floor and against the wall, kicking holes in doors and walls and cupboards, ripping the door off the fridge and throwing still-good eggs out the now-broken window, not caring where they landed, pausing only twice to go back to Dave's apartment to change music. He had some sense of fun from using a tall floor lamp to joust with TV and stereo equipment, knocking the rich fuck's toys around and popping a gaping hole in the thirty-two inch Sony, but everything else just felt perfunctory, almost like he was only doing his duty.

Finally he could feel sleep coming on. Too tired to stumble back across to his bed, he slugged back the last of his beer and then collapsed face-first on the couch, boots still on, and fell into a deep but restless sleep.

The remote stink of hydrocarbons told her that no vehicle was currently operating near this obscure piece of road. Tuning her ears, she could hear the distant clamor of people as they made their noisy way out of the city, but could hear nothing close by that might signify danger.

A blink and she knew that it was time to gather another message. Ship had told her earlier that Sniffers had been seen in the sky above this city, and that they should not take the chance that they were just passing over, but rather assume that they had settled in for a more intensive search. Happily, the strange layouts of human cities gave Ship an idea, one that she was now about to try.

Simple radio signals were out, that was certain. Even riding one scrambled signal on top of a human broadcast would likely be detected within a few hours of use as her pursuers utilized the sensitized *Latha* brains to wade through all radio traffic, looking for telltale signs. And sending signals through the human's network of coaxial cable or telephone conduits would again leave too high a likelihood of detection, even if it did come a day or two later. She was too far away from Ship to use a remote nerve complex, darts of nerve tissue fired from Ship and homing in on her and feeding her the latest information in quick bursts.

the umbilical appears a wise one, as it seems to be finding its way to completion without fault. As well, any guilt you felt must surely be tempered by the events since the alliance ship arrived.

The enemy above us continues to destroy portions of the Earth as it confirms your absence in those areas. Western California, a map showed her where, *was obliterated yesterday, and local radio states that two more pieces of the Moon are gone. You should see that by tonight it has likely broken up and begun to spin into a closer orbit. I shall assume that this means they are soon ready to give up on finding you and will have to start again; once pieces of the Moon start falling to Earth, the destruction will no longer be so fine-tuned. We must, if I may be so bold, take our leave before then, no matter the cost.*

I have another animal called a muskrat waiting in the river at the base of the drainage pipe, continued Ship, showing her a small mammal swimming in a deep pond. Strange music played and she could hear a distant voice, a human, talking about something called a hinterland who's who. *I picked this up after tapping into the local broadcast system some months ago,* said Ship. *It seems safer to utilize native fauna. Message proteins are in your system and waiting to carry back word that you received this communiqué, so please cause your finger to bleed into the water. The muskrat will receive them and carry them back to my hiding place. And there will be other animals along the way, ready to help you on your path in case of minor difficulties; this world truly was a wonder of diversity.* The use of past tense sounded bitter, even a touch forlorn.

"Thank you, Ship." She bit open the tip of her finger, shook blood into the water. "I will be back with you soon."

The urge to piss finally got Mark up from his position face down on the dickhead's couch. He blinked a few times, fighting to remove the blur from his eyes, then checked his watch; close to five in the afternoon already. With a groan he rolled off the edge of the couch and slid to his knees, stayed there for a few seconds while he looked inside himself for balance, then stood and knocked over a not-quite-empty bottle of beer on his way to the door and across the hall to Dave's apartment, unbuckling his jeans as he staggered to the bathroom. Somewhere his mind was clear enough to question why he didn't just let fly on the carpet, but he figured sometimes old habits really did die hard.

After what seemed like a ridiculously long time pissing, he washed his hands and face and ran some cold water over the stubble of his normally closely shaved head, then went into the kitchen and 'waved some two day-old coffee, still quietly surprised that the power hadn't given up. He put a little peanut butter on some bread from the fridge, grabbed an apple and cut away the brown spots, then took the food and the coffee out into the living room and sat on the big chair that looked out the window.

There were still a few people out on the streets, maybe two dozen at best, but most of them were being accompanied by soldiers or police, probably idiots who'd gassed trying to stay in the city. He could see the odd green truck or white cop car driving some roads and bridges on both sides of the river, but otherwise it was quieter out there than he could ever have imagined, deader even than downtown on a Sunday morning.

Now it was almost six; he'd really pissed away the majority of this day. Most of the gang had probably been rounded up by the cops or soldiers by now, but there was still hope one or two of them would still be around. He finished the apple with a couple quick bites then turned around and hurled the core out the open front door, where it ricocheted off the asshole's door jamb and bounced down the hall. He swallowed the last of the coffee, stuffed the peanut butter and bread into his mouth, then grabbed a pile of clothes off the floor and changed; socks and runners, frayed jeans in deference to the cool winds, SNFU t-shirt, ratty old leather jacket, and Walkman tucked in the inside pocket of the jacket, tape ready to play but tuned to the radio right now. He checked to make sure his footbag was in the right hand pocket of the coat, then grabbed his board and headed for the stairs.

There was no one in the lobby when he got there, but he figured it would be safer to go out the back door nonetheless. It opened onto an alley and provided good cover with two big dumpsters and a recycling bin, enough to hide behind if the cops or army boys drove by. The door shut quietly behind him, and Mark stepped lightly over to the nearest dumpster, holding his board and listening. A distant truck was rumbling along some road, its engine echoing in the empty spaces, but he could hear nothing close by.

Mark dropped his board to the pavement and hopped on, pushing hard with his right foot to get up a good head of steam. Still no sounds as he approached the road, and a quick look in both directions showed nothing. He caught air going off the curb and landed sweet, angled himself for the hill leading down into the river valley.

Most days when things weren't so fucked-up Mark and just about everyone he knew hung out at the old Gazebo, bumming smokes from each other, kicking around a footbag, maybe asking around for spare change or else sweeping the walk in front of a store for a couple of bucks. But that was a definite write-off now, and so he and his friends usually met at the old fire pit down below the High Level Bridge. It was well hidden but easy to get to, not far from a closed-off service road near the river and a quick stumble down a steep wooded trail from above. The problem now was that the past couple of days Mark had been by himself, waiting for anyone to show up.

A couple hundred meters down the road Mark jumped his board at the curb again, flipped it with his feet and caught it while running, crashing into the trailhead in the bush and using his other hand to grab hold of a tree to help slow him down. He paused to catch his breath, then started to pick his way down the trail towards the fire pit, expecting to be on his own again.

She was in a fairly heavily wooded area, testing the air and waiting for the best moment to cross the road and descend into the next section of trees. Human vehicles were not far away, but the winds were uncertain and the topography of this river valley made it difficult to pinpoint any noises. This seemed to be the safest spot to cross, though, with plenty of distance in both directions so that any surprises would still be far enough away to be safe. And time was of the essence now.

She dashed out onto the pavement, was not quite halfway across when she heard a voice shouting at her to stop. She picked up her pace, hoping to make it into the trees and get out of sight before whoever it was got to her, heard the loud crack from uphill and felt the bullet as it punched into the back of her left shoulder. She grunted, a great rush of expelled air, stumbled and tripped over the curb, falling head over heels down the slope and into the trees.

The agony was intense, worse than anything she'd felt since taking this form. A tree stopped her tumble a short distance down the hill, and she stayed there for a few seconds, finding her breath and concentrating on leaving behind the pain. When her eyes could focus again she looked down at her shoulder, saw a growing stain of blood, yellow smearing to orange against the gray of her shirt.

There were shouts from above now, several soldiers calling to each other as they reached the point in the road where she had been shot. Carefully, she pulled herself up and looked, could not see anyone above her, then turned and began to navigate her way as quickly as she could down the hill, using her good shoulder and arm to ricochet off of trees, letting branches and thorns slap her in the arms and face and twigs jab at her eyes and nose and forehead. Behind, still more shouting, and leaves and branches crashing as one or more of the human soldiers took up pursuit.

Mark stood just outside of the circle of logs surrounding the firepit, bouncing his footbag on the outside of his right foot, then flipping it up in the air and catching it on the top of his head before letting it slide down his back. He tried to connect with his heel to bring it back over top but missed, looked over his shoulder to see it plop to the ground, tiny cloud of dust barely showing in the combination of twilight and heavy cloud before disappearing in an errant breeze. The wind still blew hard at the trees, but they and the side of the hill protected him nicely here.

It had been another evening of being alone, waiting in vain for anyone to show up. Mark supposed that by now everyone had been bagged. He would need to find something else to do with his last couple of days left alive.

His stomach was growling now. Time to think about heading back to the apartment, get a bite and suck back a beer.

There was a loud CRACK! from up the hill just then, echoing briefly before being drowned out by a fresh gust of wind. Followed by distant shouting and then the sounds of someone crashing through the trees, coming down the hill towards him.

"Fuck!" said Mark, jumping back to the trees, away from the firepit; too late, he realized he'd left his board sitting by the logs. But before he could think to grab it or get himself hidden he heard a voice from behind him, footsteps as whoever it was dashed out of the trees.

"Help me! Please!"

A girl's voice. Mark turned, saw that he sort of knew her, a girl who'd been new on the street just a month before the aliens. Jenny. Her eyes were wide, her face looked like hell after the run through the woods, and in the fading light Mark could see the beginnings of a dark spot near her left shoulder. She seemed to be favoring that arm.

From up the hill he could hear more voices, soldiers or cops as they chased after her. He made a decision, nodded and waved to her to follow. They ran into the woods together, he running by memory but still stumbling over roots and bushes, trying his best not to whip branches into her face.

They ran for a couple of minutes, then when they could hear no signs of pursuit, walked at a fast pace. Jenny didn't complain about the bullet in her shoulder, and Mark so no other reason to talk yet. Maybe once they knew they were free of the assholes carrying the guns.

Twice it rained briefly, torrential amounts of water dumping from black clouds. In between, the clouds parted for a few short moments, and looking up through a gap in the trees Mark saw that the Moon was no longer in one piece, that what remained of it consisted now of nothing more than a few large and probably lots of small separate chunks.

"They're drifting apart," said Jenny, standing behind him and breathing hard. "Some will break up and fall into a short-term orbit, but the most of the damage will be caused by the larger pieces that spiral in."

"Big shit from space," said Mark. "Been there, seen the movie." He listened, still could not hear any sounds of soldiers; they'd probably run straight on, expecting Mark and Jenny to carry on to where the trail led to the next park along the river valley. But before he could ask her what she was going to do about the bullet hole in her shoulder, she was walking again, veered off at almost a right angle to the direction they had been heading. Startled, Mark watched her fade into the night and leaves before chasing after her.

She knew the human male from her time living among them. Mark was his name, and she recalled that he had had the respect of most people of his age group. He was fair and honest to them, if not so much to the adults that surrounded him and yet paid him almost no attention. Human traditions regarding their young were strange in this culture, but she supposed that if most people were like Mark then such traditions proved themselves out.

Oddly, though, her experiences seemed to show that most people, adult or youth, were *not* like Mark. Sad that she would never be able to discover the reasons why.

He was following her now, which came as something of a surprise. She wanted to turn and tell him to leave her be, but she was late and she was hurting more than she thought possible. Then again, she *had* asked him for help.

A small insect bumped up against her cheek and then two more times against her lips. She opened her mouth and it flew in, heading down her throat before she could even swallow.

Fewer proteins in a body this size, said Ship. *Smaller message. You are late. The lights are out already. A pigeon, a squirrel and a cat are waiting to escort you. Please stick out your tongue when the moth lands on your nose. It will gather information on your status from the saliva.*

She blinked as a fresh wave of pain and nausea washed over her, fought it off, and walked on, waiting for the moth.

They were walking the edge of the tree line now, staying close to the darker shadows in case anyone should still be patrolling down here.

The wind didn't gust as bad down here by the trees, and the rain hadn't returned. Mark was looking up at the clouds when Jenny suddenly stopped, and he had to do a little dance to the right to avoid crashing into her.

She had a moth on her nose. Her tongue was sticking out, and the moth was sitting there face down, apparently eating off her tongue.

"Aw, fuck!" Mark spun around, looking to see if any of the soldiers might miraculously appear out of the trees right now. "You're that alien chick!"

She nodded, eyes wide and tongue still out. With a whir of fluttering wings, the moth launched itself from her face and transcribed a dizzy path through the air in the general direction of downtown. Then she lurched to a start again, favoring her wounded arm and doing her unconscious best to imitate the moth's erratic attempt at a straight line. Mark followed, skipping sideways every time she threatened to fall into his path.

"I am," she finally said. They were nearing the transit bridge, and Mark half-noted that the lights on the pedestrian walkway underneath were not shining. "I notice you haven't tried to kill me or turn me in yet."

Mark shrugged. "Thought about it for a second. But we're fucked no matter what I do, right?"

Jenny nodded, a move that caused both her and Mark to wince, Jenny for the physical pain, Mark for the realization that maybe his nihilism didn't run as deep as he thought. It was a surprise to find that hope still occupied a small corner inside.

He swallowed, took a second to regain his composure. "I remember my folks sending the cops after me a couple of times, before my dad finally told me to fuck off and never come back. Shitty thing to happen to anybody, even when you have assholes for parents. At least I had a brother I could crash with sometimes, not like a lot of the others."

"I know," said Jenny. "I met some of them. It always surprised me how they got by, and how they could be so easily ignored." She stumbled as she finished speaking, and Mark reached out and caught her. She gasped, but leaned into him for a moment. "I might not make it."

"We going to cross the bridge?" asked Mark. She nodded. "No problem then. I'll help you, then you can tell me where to from there."

They walked in silence for a moment, listening to the wind rattle the aspen leaves overhead, watching and listening for any sign of more soldiers. The slate of the sky had faded to black now, except for the remaining lights of downtown reflecting off the bottom of the fast-moving clouds.

"How'd they do it?" Mark asked.

"Do what?" Jenny kept her head down, concentrating on making sure she kept from pitching over and dragging Mark down with her.

"All that crap." Mark waved his arm in a sweeping arc. "Make California disappear, tear the Moon apart, lower the sea level, swipe Japan. You know, stuff designed to make all of us shit our pants."

Jenny looked up at the dark sky for a second. "Virtual antiparticles," she said. "Controlled and focused by a genetically engineered race of creatures called the *latha*. They are working with another race of beings to find me."

Mark shook his head. "I have no fucking idea what any of that means, and I don't think I want to bother to try."

They were at the bridge now. Mark couldn't see any signs of movement, no dark shapes coming out of the shadows, no butt lighting up while a soldier took a drag. Holding Jenny tight around the waist, he started them up the twisting ramp. "What makes you so special to them?"

"I carry something both inside of me and with me. Something they desperately want to use." She glanced at him, then gritted her teeth and looked straight ahead.

Mark waited as he helped her walk, thinking she might say more. She didn't. So they walked in silence for a time, until halfway across the bridge he stopped so that she could catch her breath.

He leaned her up against the railing and then stood beside her, looking out at the lights of the city and then up at the High Level Bridge just downstream from them. The wind here was cool, but the rain had stopped for the moment.

"Something inside of you," he finally repeated.

"Too much for a human to understand," came another voice, high-pitched and a little slurred, definitely not Jenny's. Mark whirled around, not sure if he was going to try and slug the soldier, try to run, or just raise his hands in the air and give up. Maybe tell the guy that he'd found the alien chick, wounded, and was trying to find someone he could hand her over to.

But there was no soldier. Instead, a small squirrel stood on the rail just beside him, nibbling on a small seed it held in its paws. He stared at the squirrel, which finished the seed and deposited the remnants of its shell over the side of the railing.

"It is, sadly, the seed of destruction coupled with the root of discovery. The people who created this one have a sad duty to explore all that they can before entropy and chaos step to the fore. But there is no time to talk about this now," said the squirrel. It stood on its hind legs, balancing back against its bushy tail, and pointed one small paw towards Jenny. The scene felt bizarre and surreal to Mark, and then even more jarring when he saw that the animal's mouth did not appear to be moving in time with its voice. "She needs to get back to the ship, and this one is unable to help her. This one asks you to help her the rest of the way."

"Jesus," said Mark. He stood looking at the animal for a few seconds, then turned and looked back at Jenny. The talking squirrel had for a second made her seem even more alien to him, but then seeing her leaning against the railing, fighting the pain and struggling to stay conscious, she now seemed even more human. He put his arm back around her and they started walking again, the squirrel keeping pace on the rail.

"Where are we going?" he asked.

"Her Ship is still some distance," said the squirrel. "This one was sent with two others to help her get back to it so she may try to escape."

"Two others? More squirrels?"

"No," said another voice. A small dark cat and a bird, a pigeon, stepped out of the darkness. The bird flew up from the ground and lighted on Jenny's shoulder. "This one suspects that she will not make it back to Ship even with your help," said the bird.

The squirrel chittered, and then nodded its head. "Agreed."

Jenny was weighing heavier in his arms even as the pigeon said the words. Mark stopped again, only a few paces after he had last rested, let the alien girl slide down against the railing until she sat heavily on her butt. Her eyes were closed.

"Then what do we do? I'm this far, doesn't make any sense to quit now."

"Revenant," said Jenny. It was little more than a whisper.

"This one agrees," said the cat. "Ship can connect with you on the hop over and be ready to access the vortex within moments of being notified. Pigeon must go."

The bird raised its wings, but Jenny brought a hand up. "Wait!" She opened her eyes and looked up at Mark. He sat back on his haunches directly in front of her, so that she wouldn't have to look up so uncomfortably.

"What?" he said. "I don't know what a revenant is, but if it can help you get out of here, then do it."

"Only one way to escape," she said. A tear appeared at the corner of one eye. "The vortex will displace us from this system, but the power both used and ejected is enormous."

"But . . ." started Mark, but Jenny took his hand in hers. Her palm was slick with sweat.

"Everything will be destroyed, Mark. Earth, the Moon, your sun. The . . . the obliteration footprint will probably extend a little past the orbit of Jupiter. All of these will just cease to exist." A gust of wind blew her hair around her face. Mark gently removed it with his free hand.

"I can take you with me, Mark. We have samples already, things that Ship has collected during the time we've been here. Genetic material, cultural information, more. If we get out of here, Ship and I know enough to restart your race and much of your society and flora and fauna." She squeezed his hand. "It's what we do." The pain on her face was still obvious, but Mark could see a hint of a plaintive look; she was looking for forgiveness.

Mark squeezed back and tried to smile back down at her, then looked up at the dark sky to hide his growing fear. Then he shook his head. "I hope you get back safely. But I don't think I want to run away anymore. And we're already fucked no matter what happens now." He looked at the pigeon. "Go." The bird obligingly flew off, headed towards downtown.

He watched it fly into the darkness, briefly able to make out its silhouette against the lights in the abandoned office towers. "Where is your ship? Hiding underground?"

"It is the top floor of one the office buildings," said the squirrel. "That storey was replaced by Ship when they first arrived."

Mark sat down now, and watched as Jenny opened her mouth to speak, only to have a large bug of some type fly into her mouth. She looked him briefly in the eye, then closed her mouth and swallowed it whole.

You are not well, began Ship. *Inspection by the beetle before flying in indicates that the pigeon is not nearby. Therefore the assumption is made that it is flying to me to relay a message. Another bird has been dispatched in case of this scenario, and also in case this assumption is in error.*

A wide-spectrum broadcast was made by the Gyrea-Latha *alliance vessels a short while ago. It indicated that the home system had fallen to their assault, and that they now had what they needed. In their words, a vortex machine was captured whole and is currently being readied for use. Thus, they intend to destroy the Earth because they no longer require you or me to hand over our own machine.*

I believe that this is a bluff. Your genetic tailoring is every bit as indispensable as the hardware involved, and any machine captured back home will be useless without someone grown to operate it.

Both Revenants are ready for departure, and are situated such that when they take off they should prove to interest our enemy long enough to effect a proper escape. As well, the umbilical has been successfully regrown enough to allow proper access to the vortex, which as you know means we can make the escape with only minimal threat to ourselves. I know that your moral compass has changed while living among these humans, but understand that the choice was made for you long ago. And be proud that we have managed to gather as much on this civilization as we have.

If you are unable to make it to me under your own power or with the help of the human, then hopefully you have used the pigeon to relay that information. If that is the case, expect my arrival shortly.

She opened her eyes and once again looked at Mark. He sat across from her with a worried look on his face. Just then the sky lit up with the fury of a thousand lightning storms, although there wasn't a sound to be heard above the steady wind. The first Revenant had taken off and been found.

"I'm sorry," she said.

Mark watched the sky light up with frightening intensity, the flickering glow showing through the thick and heavy clouds like nukes viewed through a paper towel. He squeezed his eyes shut to protect them from the harsh light, then opened them again to see Jenny pulling herself up.

"Come with me," she said, taking his hand as he stood.

He shook his head, and then the sky lit up again. He could hear distant rumbling now. And then, silhouetted against the warring skies, a giant rectangular shape seemed to race out of the sky, easily cutting a slice out of one of the pillars supporting the High Level bridge opposite them as it plummeted into position, then coming to a sudden stop, now hanging in the air only a few feet away. It still looked like the top floor of an office building.

Jenny pulled herself over the railing and dropped before Mark could do anything to help her. But she was caught gently, by a force field or a giant invisible hand for all Mark knew, and was quickly drawn into her Ship.

Everything went horribly bright for what may have been just a fraction of a second, and then the darkness was complete.

Read The Song of the Dodo *by David Quammen, my favorite author. Inspiration was derived from that book, and many new paths were suggested. The alien, of course, was my own idea, as aliens in Quammen's writing tend to take the guise of non-native species. Now I hold out hope that some day I'll be able to go to Madagascar, in time to see some of the remarkable life that exists there before we snuff if out.*

ISLAND OF THE MOON

Jean-Chry jammed on the ancient Land Rover's brakes, flinging me forward into my shoulder belt and snapping me back to the present. Before I could speak, he had jumped from the Rover and opened the hatch. I leapt out and ran around to the back as well, reached over the Malagasy guide's shoulder as he dug around and pulled out the case holding my quick-and-light gear.

The alien *buhsik,* Ulohtsa, stepped out from the back seat as we both rummaged through our bags. He stood beside me and whistled an interrogative through his broad nasal passages. The sheen of nano devices covering his face and body made him look like someone far away on a hot day, an effect that always unsettled anyone who stared too hard at it. The devices were obviously still sampling and screening new native microfauna, and had seemed especially busy ever since our departure from New York three days ago.

But images of Ulohtsa I had plenty of, and I had no idea what Jean-Chry was up to, so besides acknowledging the alien with a small wave I pretty much ignored him this time. I had the palmcorder ready to go, disk in place, battery at full power and solar panel drawing energy to extend its life. I activated the IR receiver on my sunglasses, flicked to wide angle and held the camera in close to Jean-Chry, who continued rummaging around, cursing in three languages. Finally, he found the object of his search, a long rifle with a battered scope. Apparently the holstered pistol at his waist would not serve his purposes.

I trained the camera on Jean-Chry as he checked to make sure the gun was loaded. What did he intend to shoot? Nothing but red-brown hills covered with a thick, irritating haze from hundreds of fires and some pathetic crops here.

Jean-Chry sighted with the scope. I stepped behind and sighted along with him, zoomed the camera in on a tiny motion in some scrub a dozen meters off the road. A small gray cat stepped out, something tiny and bright green in its mouth. The cat looked briefly at us before padding off to our right. Jean-Chry tracked it with the gun.

Still focused on the cat, I said, "You're not gonna—"

The rifle's report made me jump and launched several dozen birds screeching into the air before they settled back down to their assorted perches. Behind me Ulohtsa grunted.

On the heads-up I saw the cat lifted into the air by the force of the bullet. It dropped to the ground and lay still. A hundred meters up the road two *tanala* men carrying rifles stopped and watched for a few seconds, their weapons at the ready, then carried on. I couldn't imagine where they might have seen one of the aliens before, but perhaps Ulohtsa's ebony skin made him seem less out of place here than back home.

Jean-Chry walked briskly over to the cat; I followed, Ulohtsa's long legs keeping him hot on my heels, went back again to wide angle and circled Jean-Chry as we walked. The Malagasy man looked grim.

He squatted over the cat's remains, his rifle across his knees. The cat lay there, eyes wide open and pale pink tongue hanging over yellow-white teeth, but everything from its chest on down nothing but a red stain in red earth, shattered bones and organs showing to the world. Already several flies crawled about. I focused in on the flies, on the cat, then followed Jean-Chry's hand as he reached for its mouth.

He pried the cat's jaws apart and lifted a tiny bright green lizard between his thumb and forefinger. He held it up for the camera, dangling it by its tail.

"Chameleon," said Jean-Chry. One of its punctured goggle-eyes oozed fluids, and its neck was broken. "Not as badly rare, this one, not yet. But cats and rats and pigs, people brought them here, they cause deadly damage to many things." He carried the chameleon back to the Rover. I stumbled backwards ahead of him, recording as Jean-Chry talked. Knowing now when I wanted him in the picture and when not, Ulohtsa fell into step beside me.

"Pigs run loose, like cats become . . ." He searched for a word. "Feral. Pigs eat anything, they are very bad for eggs of ground-dwelling birds. Cats, they climb trees, get the eggs and birds the pigs can't, as do rats. At least eleven species of bird are extinct since the turn of the century, five or six chameleon and at least one gecko." He gently placed the dead chameleon in a cooler in the Rover. "People brought these animals," Jean-Chry repeated, getting back into his seat.

I did the same. "But what about local carnivores?" I got in and buckled up, kept the camera on him. "What about the indigenous mongooses . . . mongeese?"

Jean-Chry smiled a bit, steering around potholes as he talked. "Once, not long ago, Madagascar had four types of mongoose; only two remain, one so rare that it may not live in the wild anymore. The fossa," he pronounced this *foosh,* "has vanished, unless you believe reports of a last pair in a few scraps of forest high in the western hills.

"But when they were here, there was a *balance.* Plenty of land to live on, no diseases to catch, no strange predators to worry about. My people have a saying: *Miova andriana miova sata. When you change kings, you change customs.* The animals on this island do not know that saying. When the new predators came, local species had no way to adapt—they could not figure how to change their customs."

He fell silent, concentrating on the road. I shut off the camera and leaned back in my seat.

We rode in silence, the landscape drifting by as I looked for more potential shots. Dilapidated shacks, men and women with guns, scrawny cats, children playing in the dirt, a constant stream of views of a world alien to both Ulohtsa and me, but one that began to look monotonously the same as we traveled.

One town bled into the next as we descended the mountain towards the park entrance. Everywhere buildings sat open to the street, markets vending giant grapefruits, durian, bananas, French bread, vegetables, samosas and more, much of it imported now, including those ridiculous raffia nut necklaces and plant holders that had been common even in Tana.

"Ambotalehy," said Jean-Chry.

"Pardon?"

"Ambotalehy, the name of this town. *Ambo* means village, *votalahey* means tombstone. Appropriate name so close to where you're going."

"A contraction," said Ulohtsa, his first words since meeting Jean-Chry at the airport.

"Pardon?"

He matched my stare. The fine dark gray hairs around his patchwork eyes ruffled in the breeze beneath his protective layer, nostrils flaring as he caught and detailed all the scents around him. "A contraction," he said.

"Right. What did you mean?"

Ulohtsa grunted. "Humans have a propensity for contracting words, Mick. This habit held up our arrival by over two of your years while we compiled new speech analogs. It is interesting to note that place names may be contracted as well."

"Uh-huh. Very interesting, Ulohtsa." I pulled out my notepad, looked for the town on the map I called up on the screen. "How far is it from here?"

"We're about six kilometers from the old park gates." Jean-Chry flashed a smile. "And then there is the walk."

"Of course." A dilapidated garage was on the right, *Pneumatique* sign in faded blue letters advertising a garage and tire shop, two young men sitting on the hood of a tire-less Nissan truck, two more leaning against the door, all with ancient battered rifles strapped over their backs, all drinking Three Horses beer and laughing at someone's sarcastic remark as our Rover strained by in first gear.

The Land Rover sped up as we left the town, bumping and scraping along the road as it descended towards the park. The smoke was much thicker. Rice paddies stepped up the sides of the mountains here, shriveled and faded banana trees occupying whatever tillable land remained.

A vicious hole dropped the truck, jamming my tail-bone into the underpadded seat, and then slamming my head into the roof as it bounced back. I groaned and turned to Jean-Chry, giving him such a look of pain and exhaustion that the Malagasy field station employee grinned again. "Soon," he said, then arched an eyebrow. "Really," which brought a grunt from the back seat. A couple of hours of this was obviously also getting to Ulohtsa.

A truck approached from the opposite direction, and Jean-Chry eased the Rover to the edge of the road to let it slip by. Scraps of timber rested in its bed, guarded by two men carrying shiny but old Kalashnikovs. I turned to watch as we drove by. Ulohtsa also watched its passage.

"That was wood on that truck, yes?" asked the alien.

Jean-Chry nodded. "Compared to everywhere else, there is a lot of wealth in Ranomafana, and these people know it. Once they worked with the park, watched money come in from tourists. But since the civil war, we get only a very few scientists, almost no journalists. No one else."

"The wood comes from the park then?"

"*Oui*. Or its edges. Few trees anywhere else, but very hard to get other sources of fuel." He swung the truck around another two potholes and more armed pedestrians. "Close now," he said, pointing ahead with his chin. "Look."

Ahead, far down the steep road, I could now see through the haze of smoke where red and poisoned farmland bled into green forest. "Trees," I said, startled at the sight.

"Ranomafana," agreed Jean-Chry. "*Ny hazo tokano tsy mba ala.*" He grinned, but it was a harsh look, not a happy smile. "That means: *One tree doesn't make a forest.* Only three preserves left in my country, and this is the smallest one. You know Perinet, what we call *Analamazaotra,* and far north there is *Andapa.* "He said these with the last *a* sort of silent, what I had learned to be a sometime Malagasy quirk of pronunciation. *Ranomafana* pronounced *Ranomafan, Sifaka* pronounced *Shih-fahk*. It was taking some getting used to, after studying all the spellings so that I could get my uploads right. Jean-Chry swung the wheel around to avoid another large pothole. "Everything else is gone, and the dying continues."

I concentrated my gaze on the small preserve, thinking of approach shots. It looked brilliant and yet pathetic, like a small emerald island in the middle of a wave-tossed, shit-brown sea. Smoke from fires rose from at least forty perimeter locations. Perhaps a little later I could float the blimp for an aerial. The park itself had been over forty-one thousand hectares when it was created, but satellites now showed only about twelve thousand hectares left. *Tavy,* the slash-and-burn agriculture of this country, had combined with the recent civil war to pretty much do in everything.

Ulohtsa leaned forward. "Different, and yet not unique. Much like your own country, Mick, a small portion of wildland in the midst of technological destruction. Although the tall gleaming structures you view as signs of an advanced state do not appear to exist on most of this land mass."

I nodded. Editorializing was the alien's strong suit some days, but on this I agreed.

And then we were rounding over another little rise and there was a building on the side of the road, less than five hundred meters away. More patchy woods accompanied by some scrub and barren red soil marched from the section of forest we had just come from right to the well-defined boundary of the park, just past the building. Jean-Chry lowered gears with a shuddering shift change, and I turned on the camera and leaned out the window, hanging on for life with one hand while shooting with the other. The stabilizer couldn't get rid of all the jumping and bouncing, but a few quick cuts of this would add to the sensation of being in a strange world, like astronauts driving our rover on the Moon.

The smoke thinned here. The structure we were approaching had a stone front and thatch roof, and two Malagasy men sat on the steps. Parked a few meters opposite was a blue-and-rust Jeep even older-looking than the Rover. A low wire fence marched along the tree line as far as I could see, warning signs in three languages posted every few dozen meters. The plants were palms, ferns, orchids, dozens more. A dizzying riot of green and the rest of the rainbow after so much red and brown. Not far from the building ran a creek, water almost clear instead of running red with eroded soil, and a small bridge crossed over. Below the bridge stood seven women, watching us drive down, taking a break from doing laundry on the rocks.

I focused on the Jeep, then pulled my head back, startled. Three men watched us approach, one in the driver's seat, one getting out of the passenger's side and carrying a rifle, and one standing in the open back, training a large mounted machine gun on the Rover. After a second's hesitation I zoomed in, got a tight shot directly down the barrel of the gun and then panned back up to the gunner's face.

Jean-Chry stopped next to the Jeep, opened the door and stepped out. Ulohtsa and I followed him, my camera still recording.

Jean-Chry shouted something in what I assumed was the Malagasy tongue, and the man who was carrying the rifle shouted something in return. Nothing angry, it seemed, just shouts of greeting. When they were face to face, our guide said a few more words and gestured for me to put down the camera.

"This is Rico," said Jean-Chry. "Rico, this is Mick." The man he had been talking to nodded, not smiling now. "Rico is in charge of the park patrol for this entrance of Ranomafana and the area around it."

"Very pleased to meet you," I said, sticking out my hand.

Rico shook my hand very gently, almost tentatively, and said, "And I am pleased to meet you, sir. I will do my best to make sure that your stay in our park is as safe as possible."

"Thank you," I said, not sure what he meant by this. The war was still a strong memory, but I had kind of hoped that being in a park would be protection enough.

"And this," said Jean-Chry, "is Ulohtsa." The alien bowed, but kept his hands to his sides.

Rico briefly nodded his head, then opened the door of his Jeep and reached into the glove compartment to pull out a small pouch that jingled with the sound of heavy coins. "Rico and his men have to have some guarantee of how they are paid to guard the park," said Jean-Chry.

"The government pays no one outside of the major centers anymore, so Duke University and some other foreign groups make sure that equipment costs and part of salaries are paid."

"And they agree to the tithe that my men and I charge to make sure that everyone inside the park remains safe," said Rico, smiling as he opened the pouch.

"He means that they look the other way, as long as Rico helps keep the park safe from the *tavy* and from poachers and thieves." Jean-Chry was smiling too. "Did you bring the coin?"

I blanked. Coin? Was I being asked to pay a bribe?

Ulohtsa coughed, a wet, gurgling sound. "I am sorry to interrupt, Mick, but I believe he means a South African gold krugeraand. Is this correct?"

Both Jean-Chry and Rico nodded.

"Ah," said Ulohtsa. "Then I was informed about this, evidently something they did not share with Mick." He held out his hand, palm up, six long and supple fingers equal in length and with the two on the outside both opposable, set at the end of a long and slender four-jointed arm. As all three of us watched, a large gold coin appeared to rise from inside the palm of his hand, like a pat of brilliant butter floating to the surface of tar soup. Jean-Chry and Rico both stood, mouths hanging open, but I had seen similar tricks before and, as soon as the coin was reconstituted, snatched it from his hand and gave it to Rico with a smile.

Rico gripped the coin but did not bite it, dropping it into the bag and then pulling two plastic badges out of a pocket. One he clipped onto my vest, the other he handed to Ulohtsa to clip to the New York Rangers t-shirt the *buhsik* liked to wear. Each badge featured a map of Madagascar in red, with a small splotch of green representing the park. Our names were crudely written with felt pen along the top of the badge.

"Keep this on you at all times," said Jean-Chry. "It carries a GPS unit and an additional tracking device, in case you get separated from us."

Jean-Chry climbed into the Rover, started it up and goosed it around to the side of the building, with Ulohtsa and myself walking casually behind. The two men sitting on the porch watched for a moment, then returned to their conversation.

We removed the gear from the Rover, threw on our packs and adjusted the straps. I left behind the blimp-and-tether line as too bulky. I could float it for shots when I came back, use it for a follow-up to the live satellite feed.

And then we were ready. Rico waved and grinned as we walked away from the building, the driver of the Jeep nodding and the man standing at the machine gun giving no attention to us but rather gazing off down the road. I brought my camera back up and recorded as we crossed the bridge and entered the forest, leaving the desolate red and burning landscape for the wealth of green and life in Ranomafana. The women doing laundry smiled and waved as I focused on them, and then turned back to their work.

The trees soon closed in on us, a canopy of branches and leaves that almost immediately shut out the now distant Martian landscape of the rest of the island. We walked in silence for a time, listening to the calls of birds and animals that broke like piercing waves against our ears.

The research camp was about two hours in, according to Jean-Chry. "But when we reach the camp it is likely that we will continue down to the actual site, although that hike is not so long." Our trail consisted mostly of volcanic cinder, and the especially steep portions had steps carved into them, sticks laid down to keep the soil from crumbling underfoot. There were a lot of these steeper sections, and I took the lead, followed by Ulohtsa and then Jean-Chry, who would only rarely shout a calm warning about the path. Ulohtsa carried nothing, of course, as all his needed universe was coating his skin, and the same nano systems somehow made for an excellent motor and strength support unit, allowing him to handle walks like this despite the strange joints in his long skinny legs.

We took several breaks, primarily for me to rest and rehydrate. My water bottle had been replenished in one of the myriad creeks and waterfalls here, filter in the canteen presumably guarding from disease and parasite. Aside from several exotic-looking birds and any number of insects and small reptiles, I saw no wildlife. Certainly no lemurs, although once Jean-Chry assured me that we had just heard the call of one type of the prosimian.

After slightly less than the predicted two hours we came upon a small and relatively flat clearing bordered by dense stands of trees on three sides, with a small, rocky stream flowing through the middle. In the clearing squatted a small foam-form hut, two large tents underneath thatch huts held up by four robust posts, three more identical thatch-roofed enclosures, one with a blue tarp hanging over one side, protecting from the elements what looked like a lot of scientific equipment, and three people sitting around a smoky campfire, a woman of East Indian appearance and the other two Malagasy men, both of them bent over a board game, pausing briefly to look as we strolled into the camp.

The woman came to greet us. I put down my camera and clipped it to my belt; I could shoot this setting later, probably under better light. It was only mid-afternoon now, the light too greedy, shadows too harsh, to get any really good shots.

"Hello, Jean-Chry," she said, smiling. He nodded in return. Then she turned to me and shook my hand. "I'm Donna Chandrapaul. You must be Arthur Mickelson."

"Mick," I said. "Please call me Mick."

Next she turned and bowed to Ulohtsa, who bowed in return. She was prepared, that much was for sure. "I am very pleased to meet you, Ulohtsa," she said.

"As I am pleased to meet you, Donna," replied the alien. "I have read with great interest all your published research about your work on this island."

I raised an eyebrow at this piece of news, and Donna nervously smiled before giving me a glance that seemed to ask if she was being put upon. All I could do was shrug.

Donna was a fairly short woman, a bit less than one and a half meters, and a little on the heavy side. Her jet black hair was pulled back in a fairly loose ponytail, and her smile was large and dazzlingly white. She wore jeans and a yellow cotton t-shirt and a light blue denim ball cap. A button phone sat on her shirt pocket, and she wore a waist pack that held two water bottles and some anonymous equipment.

Seeing me look at her pack, she pulled out and pressed a button on a small object that looked similar to the remote control for my camera. A green light momentarily flashed before fading back to a dull orange.

"He's not in the best of shape," she said, pointing over my shoulder to a distant point in the forest. "But he is sleeping right now, I think. He would normally be eating at this time, but I'd say he's probably down to his last hours now. I was actually just about to head down."

"Are there any people watching him?" asked Ulohtsa.

She shook her head. "Not at the moment, no. He's been implanted with five micro sensors, one of which has also until this morning been doing a time-release of some drugs to help keep him going. He's also being followed by three spiderbots loaned to us by MIT, so we'll know when the time comes and make sure we're there. He's only about thirty minutes from here. But if we miss it, then there's enough gear in place to get the info we need."

"Thirty minutes," I said, stretching and yawning. "I'll have had my fill of hiking after all this is done."

She laughed, a low chuckle that sounded a bit forced. "You're probably not used to this sort of thing, Mick. I promise you that once we're down in the clearing beside the bamboo stand, we'll stay put for a while." She turned and yelled something in Malagasy to the two men playing the game. They both raised their hands and waved without looking up.

"Shall we go? Do any of you need more water?"

Jean-Chry and I both shook our heads. Ulohtsa said, "All of my nutritional needs are carried on my person, Donna. I thank you for asking."

"Right, then," she said. "Let's get started."

The trail started off relatively easy. I did some more camera work and listened to the sounds of the forest. It was almost unbearably hot now, and my distress must have showed, because Donna called for a halt and led us all to a small patch of shade. I gulped down some water, then leaned back against my pack and closed my eyes, but not before turning the camera back on. One never knew when Ulohtsa would surprise with a conversational gambit.

Sure enough, it took him only a few seconds. "Why does so difficult a task attract you?" the alien asked Donna.

I flicked the IR receiver back on and opened my eyes, slowly turned the lens to Donna. Sometimes I could get better vid this way, not being in everyone's face.

Donna seemed to know exactly what she was being asked, although I could have told her that Ulohtsa never had just one meaning for any question. "I think I decided that someone needed to be here to document this, no matter how painful it will be. We've seen these events begin to happen more often over the last ten or twenty years, but this is probably the first time we've had someone on hand as an actual witness. With Mick's help," she gestured at the camera, obviously not fooled by my reclining position, "maybe that sort of witnessing can reach a larger audience and influence some people who can make a difference."

"Why on this island then? Why not somewhere else, on continental Africa or somewhere in Asia? Even North America? There must be more of this happening everywhere."

"Of course." Donna took a sip of water. "But Madagascar is an island, so we are at least able to cut out some of the variables. There are limitations to what surprises might fall on us over time."

"I thought as much," said Ulohtsa. "My understanding of the history of Madagascar is incomplete, but I think this may shed light on the country's behavior during the recent civil war."

I sat up, keeping the camera on Ulohtsa. "And?" I prompted. It wasn't often that he attempted to add any insight; he usually just asked enough questions to draw out whatever information he wanted.

He looked at me, nostrils flaring. "Our studies of human history, coupled with our analysis of broadcasts over the years it took us to travel here, told us that localized insurrections were likely to cause massive displacement of peoples. This did not happen in Madagascar. Certainly there were tribal battles for food and land, but the movements of the local population did not match those of other countries with similar problems." He stared at the forest for a moment.

"Our suspicion is that this is largely related to Madagascar being an island, thus allowing fewer options for migration. Most people involved in the war ended up staying where they started. Obviously those killed had no say in the matter, and those sent to prisons via local courts or your World Court in Europe did move, but for different reasons. But for such a violent conflict, what humans call the status quo seems to remain. Less, of course, the continuing ecological destruction."

Donna nodded, taking one last swallow of water before putting the cap back in place. "Considering all the troubles that this island has seen, they are a remarkably civil people. Put Hutu and Tutsi from fifty years ago onto an island this size and I think they'd quickly drop each other back to the stone age."

"Too many of us, though," said Jean-Chry, looking at me. "What you and Mr. Uhlotsa will soon witness will soon enough not be an isolated event."

"But it is also a lack of options," continued my alien companion. "There are no other places to go for the people of this island, and certainly not for the animals. Sometimes . . ." Ulohtsa paused, something that he rarely did. "I beg your pardon. Sometimes even the largest island is not enough to protect you from such a disaster, and striking out over the widest of seas is the only way to learn and to save yourself. Even if all you leave behind is already lost."

He stood up, joints on his long legs snapping into place. "Shall we move on?"

We all stood as well, Donna looking at me with a bewildered expression, Jean-Chry just staring at the alien, likely wondering where such a soliloquy had come from, considering how relatively quiet Ulohtsa had been since he had met us at the airport. I shouldered my gear bag and we started off again.

The trail here accommodated two people walking side by side, so I joined Donna in front of Jean-Chry and Ulohtsa. "How long have you been working out here?"

Donna turned and grimaced at the camera. "Six years," she said. "Although I've been back to Duke and home to Toronto a couple of times, and I've visited Europe and Nairobi for some lectures and conferences."

"So you were here when the shooting started."

She nodded. "I was in the park, following some large diademed sifakas when I got a call. It was my fiancé, calling from his hotel room in Tana. There were fire-fights right outside his hotel all night and all day, and he was hiding in his room and telling me that everything was going to be all right. But then he decided to make a run for it, to try and get out of town and back to the park."

"Your fiancé. This was Dr. Mehta?"

Donna bit her lower lip, nodded. I remembered the story from when it first aired, just a small piece uploaded by a local freelancer, about a world famous primatologist who had been shot dead and his body hacked to bits, whether by rebels or government forces, no one knew.

"*Vatofalia sy vanja: isaky ny mihaona mitselatra ihany,*" said Jean-Chry, coming up and putting his hand on Donna's shoulder. Donna smiled and reached up, patted his hand with hers. "That means, *flint and gunpowder: every time they meet there is an explosion,*" he said.

Donna grinned again, shook her head. "These Malagasy, Mick, they have a saying for everything."

I smiled, a little cautiously because of the touchy subject matter. "So I noticed."

We fell into silence now, so I turned the camera back to the path ahead. The trail had quickly degenerated into a small and bumpy slice of open ground, the foliage around us thickening with every step. We now descended along something that Donna called a vane, a ridge following the slope of the volcano on which this part of the park rested, two small steps in either direction taking the errant hiker down a steep and deep fall. The trees overhead filtered the light to a shadowy blue-green, but the camera adjusted itself to give a more viewable image.

Donna took the lead and I followed as closely as possible, hoping to get some usable bites from her whenever she turned her head to say something. "Over the past few decades we've seen several species of lemur go extinct, along with many other species of megafauna the world over."

"Megafauna?"

"Large animals," said Donna. I stepped nearer and steered the lens over her shoulder to view her from the side. I could rejig the wide-angle effect later. "Lemurs are the megafauna of Madagascar, with a couple of others."

"Like the fossa?"

Donna nodded. "Megafauna and extinct. Yes."

"So how many are no longer with us?"

"At least a dozen since the turn of the century. Dozens more were lost over the couple thousand years since humans came to the island."

"What about zoos?" I asked. I knew some of the answers to these questions, but even if the net didn't use this stuff, I could edit it into a passable doc that I could sell or run privately. "Aren't any of them capable of keeping some animals, trying to save them?"

"You're thinking of the commonly known animals, the ones the zoos have budgets to work on. Charismatic megafauna that every school kid knows."

"Charismatic megafauna," I repeated.

"Good-looking animals that have great visual appeal. You ought to know exactly what I mean."

I nodded.

"Anyhow. Lots of animals are extinct in the wild now, or virtually so, and so far captive breeding programs have managed to keep them from going over the edge."

"Elephants," I said.

Donna nodded. "Good example, if not *originally* relevant to what is happening here. Latest counts peg the wild African elephant population at two hundred and thirty nine, all that remain in two parks in South Africa."

"What do you mean by 'not originally relevant'?" I misstepped as I spoke, bobbed and weaved to catch my balance. The camera stayed locked on Donna.

"We're on an island," she replied. "Continental Africa is not an island. When the elephant wandered truly wild, relatively unaffected by people, it was in a situation that promised genetic diversity and could cushion any blows to the system. But as time went on, we ate at more and more of its territory and made it impossible for one herd to move to lands where another herd might exist. Which relates nicely to what Ulohtsa was talking about earlier." She looked back at him. "You say you have read my work. Have you read MacArthur and Wilson?"

The alien huffed, but said nothing else. "That means yes," I whispered. "He sometimes acts like a human and sometimes doesn't."

"Okay. Well, back in the 1960s two men, Robert MacArthur and Edward O. Wilson, put together what came to be known as the theory of island biogeography. They basically stated that you could use math to calculate the species turnover on an island, depending on both the size of the island and its proximity to the mainland. So with a ten-fold increase in the size of the island, they showed that there followed roughly a two-fold increase in species diversity."

Splashing through a muddy puddle, I had a thought. "But what about Chaos? I thought that something as chaotic as nature wouldn't let itself be pinned down like that."

Donna smiled, pushing aside a branch. "It doesn't. But what they came up with is a good rule of thumb, an excellent jumping-off point for lots more work to come. Some people later decided that this rule fit well with what we were doing on continental land masses, that national parks were nothing but islands in and of themselves."

"So Ranomafana is an island on an island."

"Exactly! If the fossa had had a safe travel corridor from here to Perinet and to Andapa, perhaps it would still be alive. Of course, that begs the question of its having the proper prey available. Large carnivores are always more susceptible to degradation of their environment; witness DDT and raptors last century, or the grizzly bear and highways and strip mining in Canada in this one, although in this case, the grizzly is certainly the more salient point, as it was affected by loss of habitat more than poisons we released into its environment."

"So what happened to the lemurs?"

Donna had begun to get into her role here. She even brushed back her hair with one hand, smiling that winning smile at me. I smiled back. "Well, some are still alive, some in relatively decent shape. But the Golden Bamboo Lemur was a difficult case from the beginning. No one even knew it existed until Patricia Wright found it in the late 1980s, and then when it *was* found no one could figure out too much about its life, its habits. It shares the bamboo stands with the Greater Bamboo Lemur, but they have opposite cycles and eat different portions of the shoots. Numbers have always been low, though, and we had a lot of trouble keeping one alive in captivity for very long.

"The war didn't help. Its aftermath brought increased *tavy,* and some of the lemur's routes from one bamboo stand to another were destroyed."

"More islands," I said.

Donna nodded. "Island fauna are also more likely to fall prey to disease, environmental disaster, introduction of non-native predators, what have you. In our case here, we had an unidentified vector carry in a disease for which we could find no cure, one that rampaged in no time through both the tiny wild population and the insignificant captive one. As it happened, two of the lemurs from one family group of five seemed to have developed an immunity, but before we could react and collect eggs from the female, a poacher killed her. Archie, the male, is quite old, and we discovered the cancer had spread so widely through his body that it wasn't feasible to collect any sperm from him, although we have taken tissue samples and stored them at Duke and on the Faroe Islands."

"And Archie's the last one."

Donna rubbed at her eye for a couple of seconds. "He is."

We spoke seldom after, starting out on the path again and listening to the sounds around us. Donna identified some of the sounds for the camera, diademed sifakas, several birds in the trees. The sifakas, a type of lemur, were still doing okay, she said, and while tree-dwelling birds were still commonplace, almost all the ground-nesters were extinct now, killed by pigs and cats and *tavy.* She stopped often and pointed out insects, giant spider webs, frogs disguised as dead leaves, more. I consumed more water with each of these breaks, the heat building up and really starting to get to me. Ulohtsa remained as imperturbable as always.

After a pause to drink water and snack on a cereal bar, Donna turned to the alien. "Why are you here, Ulohtsa? How is it that you come so many light years and then insist on coming to this island in the middle of nowhere in the hope of seeing a spark of light fade away?"

I grimaced. Great phrasing, and I'd been so busy rehydrating I'd let the camera pause itself. I turned it back on and zoomed in on the alien's dark face. Maybe I could get her to re-ask it later, just to give his answer coherence.

Ulohtsa stood still for a moment, the only movement a slight ruffling of the tiny hairs around his eyes. And then he answered. "There are only three of my people on this world at this moment," the alien said. "Our resources may seem boundless compared to your own, but they have very real limitations; thus, we can only afford to send the very few to gratify the needs of the many.

"We will not long remain on Earth. The galaxy is impossibly large and our racial desire to touch upon as much of it as conceivable is equally impossible to gratify. As tourists, we need to see and experience, to touch and smell and taste." Here Ulohtsa paused for a moment, clasping hands together. I zoomed in on the hands, wishing to hell I had this going live. In the four years since their arrival on Earth and the three months since Ulohtsa had chosen to accompany me, none of the aliens had spoken this much or admitted exactly what they were doing here, much less his reason for wanting to come to Madagascar.

"Unfortunately," continued Ulohtsa, "these experiences must also include pain and loss. For us there is no completion without a full spectrum of the hosts' lives. While sometimes that may include only reading or experiencing your visual media, the opportunity to witness the death of an entire species was too great to miss. Indeed, the opportunity goes further, as not only does it serve as a stark warning to ourselves, it also promises to play a larger role in the story of the death of an entire planet." The alien looked me in the eye. "Please forgive me for saying so, Mick, but we see little hope for any meaningful existence for humankind beyond the next seventy of your years. Shall we continue walking now? It is important that we do not miss the passing of this creature."

We watched as Ulohtsa strode off down the path, all three of us shell-shocked. Donna looked at Jean-Chry, then at me. "Jesus Christ," she said. "I'm sorry. That was a can of worms I didn't want to open."

I shook my head. "Not your fault. You heard him. They're getting ready to leave. Maybe tall dark men from outer space also find confession good for the soul."

Ten minutes later we came down off the trail and into a small clearing that bordered on a bamboo stand. Two tents stood in the middle, along with three waterproof containers. Donna opened one and pulled out a large screen and some other equipment, Jean-Chry helping.

I stepped to the side and prepared a seven-minute report, something to run while we waited for the main event. Hell, there was enough news with Ulohtsa alone, but we had come here at his request, so I figured I should follow through with that story first.

Afterward, I set up the rest of my gear. First thing was the mini dish, which unfolded easily. I set that on the ground and then put the stand up with the dish on top of it, extending it to its full height of three meters. I unfolded my own screen, linked it to the dish, then searched the sky for the satellite. The GPS unit built into the screen gave me our location, and then transferred that information to the chip running the dish and stand. A quiet whirr emanated from it as it adjusted its position, and the signal locked.

Next I prepared the remote pod and set the smaller camera onto it. I could program in Archie's location later. After some final preparations, I sat down in the shade and relaxed.

Twenty minutes later, something in Donna's mass of equipment started to chirp wildly. Both Donna and Jean-Chry jumped to action, and after ignoring my repeated questions if this was it, Donna finally nodded and said, "Shut the fuck up and let me concentrate, Mick!"

She pulled a hand through her hair, then said to Jean-Chry, "He's not taking well to us shutting off the drugs."

I sat in front of my screen and hit the dialup hot key and waited, listening to the muted ring.

"Newsroom. Jenny speaking."

"Jenny, it's Mick. Got something coming your way mighty quick, I think. Should be live."

"Hi Mick! How are you? Is this Ulohtsa's Madagascar story?"

"I'm fine, Jenny, and yeah, I'm in Madagascar. The subject of the story is right on the edge even as we speak. Can you get a producer to clear me to break in as soon as I'm set up?"

"I think Martin is in his office right now, Mick. I'll see if I can track him down. But they're doing a live Q and A with that Russian who saw that angel on the space station. They may not want to interrupt it."

I rolled my eyes. Beside me, Donna turned and mouthed *angel?* "Just get Martin for me, Jenny, let me pitch this."

"Okay. Hang tight."

While I waited, I set the main camera on a small tripod, linked it to the screen, then pulled out my remote pod and set the smaller camera on it. Then I leaned over and looked at Donna's setup. "Do you think my screen will be able to talk to yours?"

"Likely. Why?" She didn't take her eyes off the scrolling data.

"I should have checked earlier, but just so that my remote can find its way to Archie without any trouble. Figure maybe you have the coordinates in there." I entered a command, waited for the two to hook up by IR, then asked for where the lemur was sitting right that moment, and fed that information to the remote pod, which immediately started walking towards the bamboo. Before it was at the edge I double-checked, made sure that the camera was broadcasting to the screen so that I could feed the live image back to Atlanta. Out of the corner of my eye I noticed that Ulohtsa was walking towards the remote pod, but ignored him; he knew better than to mess with my equipment.

"Mick?"

"Yeah, Martin. I'm here."

"Can you give me visual yet? We've warned Lucy to stand by; she knows that she'll have to cut this cosmonaut flake loose as soon as we give the word."

I typed in a command. "Can you see anything now?"

"Yeah, I've got a crappy view of a bunch of trees. Jesus, Mick, you'd better have something better than this."

I picked up the remote, fitted the earpiece and lapel mike, turned the screen so I could look at it, then took off my glasses. No headsup display for when I was on live. Then I switched the view to the other camera, stepped in front of the lens. "How's this?"

"Better, but barely," came the voice in my ear. "Mick, you look like shit. Can you wipe off some of that sweat?"

"Yeah, just a sec. Jean-Chry?" The Malagasy man stood and nodded; he'd started watching me once Donna had all her gear going. "Inside my pack there's a small green towel. Can you dig that out and toss it to me, please?"

Jean-Chry dug around and found it, handed me the towel and I nodded my thanks, wiped the sweat from my forehead. "Better?"

"Barely. So where are we in this?"

"Last legs. Let me just check with my expert." I turned to Donna. "Any estimates on time?"

"Not really, Mick. Maybe less than half an hour." She shook her head, from my angle looking almost despondent.

The sun was blistering hot. I wiped at my forehead again and looked back to the camera. "You get that, Martin?"

"Yeah. Split the signal for me, get me both cameras. I'll decide what to put up when." I did so. "Okay, so the remote is still walking through ... what the hell is it walking through?"

"Bamboo, trees. Rainforest."

"Okay. Looks like it's negotiating things fine. And . . . hey! What the hell is that?"

I peered at the screen. "Shit! It's Ulohtsa!"

Donna jumped up from her screen, and she and Jean-Chry stared into the bamboo stand. I knelt and took a closer look at my own screen, but couldn't tell what the alien was up to. When Donna looked at me, I shook my head and mouthed *don't worry.* She nodded dubiously.

"That fucking alien has done his best to not become the story since a week after he landed, Mick. Why the hell is he getting into the picture now?"

I shook my head, then stood back up so that the camera could see me. "I don't know, Martin. But I do have something I can run for you that will probably serve as a nice depressing scoop courtesy of the same damn alien. Problem is, I figured it wasn't related to this story right now, so it's in the camera that's walking beside Ulohtsa."

"Great. I'm interested, but you'd better get it to me fast once this is all played out. In the meantime, what can we run for background while you talk to Lucy?"

"Yeah. Just let me dig it out, slap it into the screen." I pulled the disk from my vest pocket, slid it into the screen and tapped a button. "Here it comes in a squirt. Seven minutes worth. There'll be more to come when I edit this all into a tighter piece with more salient info, but it's a good starter."

"Got it. We'll probably split the screen for when we need, but of course the viewers will have their own choices about how they want to watch anyway." He paused for a second. "You about ready to go live, Mick?"

"I'm fine."

"Great. Lucy blew off Markov and we're into a short break running along the bottom while she gets up to speed. We have that synth voice of Ted Turner breaking into other channels right now, hooking viewers over; FCC lets us strafe for five minutes. Although we still have to fight off other dead celebs, like when CBS sneaks Walter Cronkite into one of our senior specials."

"Walter who?"

"Exactly." A pause. "All right, look smart, fifteen seconds to going live!"

"Can you hear me, Mick?"

"Hi, Lucy, got you no prob."

"Three, two, one . . ."

"Welcome back," said the soft female voice in my ear. "We have a special live report coming to you via satellite from the Ranomafana National Park in Madagascar." She pronounced the *a* at the end. "Joining me now is CNN reporter Arthur Mickelson. Mick, can you tell me what's happening in Madagascar right now? This isn't anything to do with the civil war, is it?"

"Pix on you now, Mick," whispered Martin.

I gave my best serious reporter's face to the camera. "Thank you,

Lucy. No, my visit here has nothing to do with the civil war, which as you know claimed more than two hundred thousand lives over the course of two and a half years of bitter fighting. What people may not realize is that the conflict, coupled with other problems we will hear about in my report, has helped bring to the very brink of extinction many species of animal and bird. It has also contributed to the outright obliteration of several other species. Here is my report on the background of what early explorers once called the 'Island of the Moon'—Madagascar, its people, and its disappearing wildlife and wildlands." Martin whispered in my ear that the piece was now running.

I turned back to the screen, watched as the remote pod moved further into the bamboo. Ulohtsa had vanished from sight. The readout from the link to Donna's screen told me that the lemur huddled only about four meters away.

The view showed us near the edge of the grove; panning the camera showed plenty of bamboo and trees and a stream on the far right, brief glimpses of sunlight reflecting off the shallow water. Digital numbers on the bottom of the screen showed the distance as the camera closed in, slowly counting down as the pod picked its way through the thick stand of bamboo.

"There he is," whispered Donna.

The camera had tilted upwards, following the signal being relayed to Donna's screen. There on its haunches on a thick branch sat a small golden-brown animal, with immense dark eyes, large puffy and golden-brown cheeks, and small tufts of whitish hair on its ears. In behind, I could see the slight metallic glint of an out-of-focus spiderbot, still monitoring its ward.

The lemur, Archie, was breathing heavily, its tongue hanging listlessly. It blinked slowly, as if its eyelids each weighed a kilo.

"That it?" asked Martin.

"Yeah," I said. "Doesn't look too good, does it?"

"No. Jesus, cute little thing, though. Got those big doe eyes. Ted's been out strafing the nature and kid channels, and we're seeing a significant upswing in ratings already. Got the pic of the lemur running in a box in the lower left corner right now. I'd say about half are maximizing that pic and letting your piece run in the background, Mick."

I shook my head. "Thanks a fucking lot, Martin. Nothing like an ego shot from you to make my day."

He chuckled. "Think nothing of it. Hey! I just had an idea. Can we get this scientist's bio readouts patched in to your screen? We can run the lemur's heart rate and the like along the bottom of the screen, let people know just how close to croaking this thing really is."

"Enough of a death watch already, don't you think?"

"Just ask, Mick."

I sat down beside Donna. Most of the numbers on her screen were incomprehensible babble, but I did recognize the lines and numbers that showed Archie's heart rate and brain activity. "These right here." I pointed at them. "Can we patch them over to my screen? My producer wants to run them below Archie's picture."

Without looking at me, she entered a command and continued monitoring the situation. My request had pissed her off, but all I could do was lay a placating hand on her arm.

"Good job, Mick," came Martin's voice. "Looks good enough that we have Ted chasing after the medical channels now. Get ready for live again."

I wiped my forehead again and faced the camera, keeping one eye on the screen. The story was nearing its conclusion. The picture split again, allowing Lucy some more screen time. When my uploaded story ended, an image of me would replace it, at least until Archie took precedence. And allowing of course that no other story jumped to the front of the queue.

The piece wound down. "That was Arthur Mickelson with a report on the current happenings in the island nation of Madagascar," said Lucy. "We'll return to Mick now for a live report about the state of the Golden Bamboo Lemur, and possibly some information on what interest this forlorn little creature holds for Ulohtsa, the alien *buhsik* accompanying Mick during his reporting from around the globe." She turned to face a new camera. "Mick, we have a third image up, the Golden Bamboo Lemur's. Bring us up to date on the situation."

"Thanks, Lucy. Just minutes ago Dr. Donna Chandrapaul's equipment sounded an alarm indicating that the lemur, which the staff here at Ranomafana call Archie, was nearing his last moments of life. As you can see by the readouts accompanying his image, his heart rate appears to be very irregular, and he's having a difficult time breathing."

"Right. Can you update us on what Ulohtsa has been doing on this trip?"

"I've been informed the President is watching now, Mick," whispered Martin in my earpiece. "He's been told that something big is about to run."

"As you know, Lucy, Ulohtsa is a rather ... taciturn being. Aside from dealing with government officials when he and his companions first landed, he has not shared much of anything. And yet today—"

"Shit, Mick, what is that?" I turned to look at Donna, wondering why she had interrupted me. She pointed, first at my screen, and then at the grove behind me.

"Mick?" This was Lucy. "We're having some image problems."

I ignored her. On the screen, Archie had stopped moving completely, although the telltales still showed him to be alive. A blackness crept up his lower body, having already completely enveloped the branch he was sitting on. It was not a shadow, not in the light that existed in the bamboo stand. It looked more like a swarm of tiny dark ants, scaling his body and all the trees behind him.

I swung around. The same blackness was overtaking all the trees and bamboo in that grove. The real thing had little resemblance to the image on camera: no matter how high the resolution, it couldn't capture the absolute absence of light and yet show what I certainly could tell was the flowing movement of a steady, shifting mass, like millions of insects climbing over each other to gain purchase. Or flowing like black lava, except against the hold of gravity.

Lucy was running a steady commentary now, thinking on her feet even if it meant that some conjecture was wrong. But she was talking about Ulohtsa and his protective layer of nano devices, and I somehow knew that she at least had the right idea.

Black completely covered Archie now, and a few seconds later it had also obliterated the camera lens.

Atlanta quickly moved the image to a smaller box in the lower right corner; ready to come back as soon as something could be seen, but unwilling to let the viewers make up their own minds about how important that image may be.

"What's he doing, Mick?" Donna's voice had a rising edge to it, as if she was nearing her snapping point.

"I don't know," I said, gazing blankly for a few seconds. Then I remembered what I was supposed to be doing, brought my attention back to my job. "Lucy, I suspect that Ulohtsa may have something to do with all this. Certainly I can attribute it to nothing natural or even unnatural that our own world has to offer." At this point Ulohtsa came calmly striding out of the blackness, an ebony shadow detaching itself from a greater darkness.

The disk from my palmcorder rose from his hand, much like the coin had earlier. "When you broadcast this, it will explain much," said the alien. "It will play from the appropriate moment. You and our companions of the day are familiar with what I said, but your world needs to hear it, although we suspect no advantage will come to your people from hearing a message many of your own kind repeat like a mantra."

The darkness had started to fade, deep green sliding in to replace the all-encompassing black. Ulohtsa continued to speak.

"The lemur is unaffected by the swarming, and will soon give you the spectacle you desire. We felt it necessary to, if you will, remember one piece of this world above all others, and that memory will be of this place, of this day.

"I will take my leave of you now, as will my companions. This moment will serve as a fine memory, and a suitable warning for our own kind." A pause, and then, "My people live on an island as well, one which takes us to other, larger islands. Earth has been one such island. Although I believe it will not, may your island find a way to survive."

Then, to add to the day's surprises, Ulohtsa took my hand and held it for several long seconds; his touch was cool and dry. "Mick, you have been a fine traveling partner, as well as an excellent teacher and study in what you call human nature. You are to be thanked."

And then he walked away, fading quickly into the woods.

Everyone began shouting at once, Martin and Lucy in my ear, Donna and Jean-Chry beside me. To focus, I shut out the sounds and stared straight ahead, wondering where Ulohtsa's departure left me and zeroing in on Archie.

The lemur was barely hanging on. His heart rate fluctuated, crazy rhythm that made him appear to grind his teeth in pain.

"Lucy, I have Ulohtsa's story ready to go, but Archie has only minutes, if not seconds, to live."

"Shit, Mick," said Martin. "Let the fucking little monkey go. This story is way bigger!"

I zoomed in, framing the picture so that we saw the lemur and not much else. It was gasping for breath, head arched back and tongue hanging out, eyes closed to tiny slits. In response to Martin I said, "Lucy, I think what Ulohtsa intended was for us to watch this, the absolute extinction of a species, and to reflect on our involvement in that loss before delving further into any cryptic messages he may have left. Let's watch now."

Archie's eyes were closed now, breath still coming in wheezing puffs that looked capable of knocking him off his perch. He made no other sound, no other movement beyond crouching closer to the branch.

His breaths became smaller, spaced farther apart. The sun hid its face behind clouds, fat and slow drops of rain dropped on us in the clearing, and then a heavier and faster rain, enough water to begin to wet his fur through the thick roof of leaves.

He opened one eye, perhaps staring at the familiar rain for one last moment. And then he closed it again, curled up in a tight ball, shuddered slightly, and died. The last of his family, the last of his species.

Donna hugged Jean-Chry and both wept. On my screen, Lucy was wiping at her eyes. No one spoke.

I remembered then that I still had the disk. I dropped it in the player, pressed the key. As I sat on the wet ground, Donna and Jean-Chry entered the forest to retrieve Archie's body, and Ulohtsa's accusing words washed over me like the rain itself.

The opening segment tells it like it is: while living in Utah, my son Aidan, then four, sprung that very question on me. Good father that I am, I decided to make him immortal and very lonely.

THOSE GRAVES OF MEMORY

for Aidan, with love and thanks

My earliest memory is from when I was four. At least, I think it's my memory.

We were going somewhere, my father and my little brother and me, and we must have been in some kind of hurry because I was riding in the stroller with my little brother sitting in my lap. If I dig really hard, I can see shapes that might be mountains and others that are buildings, and I do remember that my mother worked at the university in one of the cities where I grew up, a city in a valley, so perhaps we were going to meet her after work.

The memory takes an odd twist here, because the only image I have of my father's face is from when he was dying, somewhere around a hundred years old, skin like old parchment and pain lining his eyes. And so I can only picture this youthful body topped by his decrepit and ancient-looking head, pushing us along.

We were moving along then, and I looked up into his face, and asked him when I was going to be sixteen.

"In twelve years," he told me.

This was a game we often played, I think, my picking an age and him telling me how long I had to wait, as if any time frame beyond Today and Tomorrow had any meaning for me. I asked him about a couple more, and then asked, "When am I going to be twenty eighty?"

Not two thousand eighty, of course, but twenty eighty. He could have taken it as a nonsensical number, but he chose to take me seriously, first telling me that it would be two thousand and seventy six years, and then telling me that that was longer than anyone had ever lived.

By chance we happened to then be walking beside a cemetery, and so my next logical question was, "When am I going to die?"

"I don't know, son," came the answer. "No one knows exactly when that will happen."

"But I want to know," I said. Thinking back on what I remember, I guess my voice was a little whiny. Likely I was tired.

My father smiled and told me that no one could know, and then leaned down to take care of something involving my little brother. And that is about where the memory ends.

I've barely thought about this over the many years, but now that I have cause to, it amazes me just how wrong my father could be.

The great mass of rock and dirt I stand on is gray and barren, cold and without any redeeming features to speak of. It barely spins on its axis, there are no geologic phenomena going on underneath its surface. Here and there are melt points, places where the rock had once started to succumb to the intense heat being thrust at it from the outside, and sad little punctuations of what this planet might once have been capable of.

I reach down and touch some of the melted rock, a kind of basaltic field, and my skin flows and adjusts itself so that I can actually feel the texture. Nothing here is really recognizable to me, but it is a small ritual that I need to be able to reconnect.

The land around me is flat, for the most part, some minor dips and bumps that lead off into the darkness. I adjust my eyes so that I can see to the horizon, but there is nothing higher than my own eyes as far as I can see.

You're sure this is the place?

I shrug. "As sure as I'll ever be. There were times when the Sentinel either died or lost its mind and had to be replaced, and during those periods I suppose anything could have happened."

A snort. My skin has nurtured its attitude over all the time we have been together. *Anything! The last Sentinel was insane and had been forgotten for over three hundred million years! The only reason anyone remembered it was that it managed such a spectacular suicide it was able to attract every sentient within five thousand light years.*

"And so maybe there was extra tectonic shift during that time, and a few unexpected earthquakes. The stresses during the journey might have been enough to make some changes. But this is close, I'm sure of it."

As sure as I'll ever be, as I'll ever be allowed. "Where is the sun now?" I ask the skin.

Six light years away, it answers. A view from away is now in front of my eyes, of this planet sliding through space and then finding another of the new folds, disappearing for a moment and then the view switching, planet reappearing like a discolored ball oozing out of a viscous oil. Looking up, I watch as the dim and distant stars disappear, and then show their faces again, new patterns showing dimly against a velvet backdrop. *Four point two light years now. It will be a little while until we can redirect the next fold into our path.*

"Have you heard from anyone else yet?" I ask, expecting a negative.

There was an inquiry from Sonja, replies the skin.

This makes me blink in surprise. "What did she ask?"

She wanted to know about time frames, a question that surprised me since it comes so late in the process.

"Why didn't you tell me?"

It only happened two folds ago. You seemed busy, lost in your memories, and I was busy supervising the fold.

"Does she sound interested?"

Perhaps. It was only the briefest of conversations, and she didn't wish to speak with you. It has been so long since we last spoke with her, much less saw her, I don't know if I would be able to read any subtle hints that she may choose to offer.

I'm walking now, trying to remember things. My brain can't possibly store all of the information it has collected throughout my life, even with its complete restructuring. And so in addition to the constant companionship of my skin, everywhere I go I am trailed by a drone, and I have set it so that every few decades it does a partial memory swap for me, permanently retrieving some memories and replacing them with others, complex random generators determining what comes back to my mind, but always leaving the core memories that help me run my everyday life. The drone is a small device that hangs in orbit when I am ground-bound or else follows me along when I am in transit or living away in the open reaches, and is in constant contact with me, always making sure to back up the memories that I create.

With a signal from the skin, the random generators are shut down, and the drone organizes my memories by rough chronological order, hopefully taking the earliest, fuzziest remembrances and finding their correct homes in the timeline of my life. I ask to remember the house I grew up in, and the city where I lived. And I wait.

After a few moments there is a brief sense of loss as I become aware that there are some things I can no longer recall. And then some other pictures come to mind, and I close my eyes and experience them for what seems like the first time since they really happened.

Once done, I open my eyes again. "Satisfactory?" I ask the skin.

Enough, it says. *I'm sure it won't be exact, and of course we aren't going to have a blue sky, but it should be close.*

I smile, and then sit down on the rock and watch. It starts slowly, a pattern establishing itself in the contours of the barren stone fields that surround me. The first to grow is the house, a single story brick structure with a driveway on the left. Even if the memory is so vague as to make this house an inexact replica, the shock of seeing it is still great, and I almost expect to see my parents and younger brother come out the front door.

Houses are now growing on either side, and further down the new street. None of them are as well formed, but all I want for this endeavor is the *sense* of home, not necessarily the real thing.

Across the street sits the parking lot and the field where I used to play, and now the nearby mountains are starting to swell up out of the earth. Trees and grass are being formed, and when I look down beside my feet I see a small toy. I pick it up, and remember it as a plastic model of a dinosaur.

Styracosaurus, says the skin. *The template has worked very well,* it continues. *Everything in the area we established has grown according to plan, so obviously the seeding did what was required.*

Another image crosses my eyes, the planet fading from view and then reappearing as it finds another fold in its path. *Just under two light years now. One, perhaps two more folds and we will be there.*

Just then everything around me gets bright, an intense light coming from up high. I look up and see what looks like a new star blazing forth, but then the skin focuses closer for me and I see that it is a small planet, just arrived through its own fold and slowing down by superheating its core and then blowing off the excess matter and energy through a newly created hole on one of its continents.

It will swing well wide, says the skin. *But it doesn't appear to have enough power to completely cut its momentum.*

The planet grows large in my vision and I continue to watch, fascinated, as it comes ever nearer, a stream of molten iron and rock shooting out ahead of it in a fiery lance, a ball of gray stone punctuating a scream of red across the entire vault of the sky. It's a good thing it has been steered to miss me; I would not be happy to have to redo every single thing when we are so close to the mark.

"Hello, Bryce."

A small smile touches my lips, sudden feeling of a sad type of joy nearly overwhelming me. "Hello, Sonja. It is so good to hear your voice again."

"And yours. Listen, I will be lifting off from here in just a few minutes, and will soon be down to join you."

"Wonderful," I say. And it is. When memories go, I often forget how much I miss human company. "My skin will forward you the coordinates so that you can land safely in the school yard. I'll meet you there."

And so I sit and wait, and continue to delve into my memories.

There were no people of any kind on the world when I arrived, but I soon received an automated signal indicating that one was on the way. It was an old-time signal, just a beacon, really, not a smart neuron evident in its message. My skin accessed some early memories from the drone for me, and soon reminded me that these beacons had existed three hundred million years before or longer, a small and dumb alarm to let the owner of a planet know when someone had arrived.

A doorbell, so to speak.

It was Sonja who came to answer the door. She had taken over the Stewardship of that particular planet after its owner-species had faded away. She had placed a fold in orbit above the planet, and so I watched as the sky opened up above me, a rend in the fabric of space that ran from horizon to horizon, and disgorged the small asteroid she was then using for her wanderings.

We had talked once or twice as well, and had met at least once before, a meeting that had happened so long before neither of us bothered to dig for the memory. It seemed more important for us to just discover each other anew at that time. All I knew was that it was a surprise to see her, that after almost a million years since my last personal contact with anyone, I wasn't quite sure how to behave. But she was able to help with that.

It seems now like it happened in the blink of an eye, but for over a millennium she and I remained on that planet. She was the last lover I ever took. Several times we considered starting a family, but a look into the sky was all we ever needed to dissuade us.

Sure, the absolute end was still some billions of years away, but it just didn't seem fair, somehow, to saddle any children with the knowledge that their future would be so limited.

"Nice place you have here," says Sonja. She's smiling, and now that the air is back in this small area, her skin has slipped away from her lovely face.

"Thank you," I reply, and reach out and take her hand.

She leans forward and gives me a kiss on the cheek. It feels a little awkward, having been so long. "Is this really where you grew up?"

I shrug. "As best as I can remember it. There was a phrase that my father taught me when I was young, something he sometimes used in school: 'Close enough for rock and roll.'"

"Ha!" Her laugh is a short, joyous bark. I have been alone for so much of my long, long life, that I have forgotten how splendid it can be to have the right company.

"You know, you could have just built a ship to come," I say to her. I'm trying to keep my voice stern, but the look in my eyes tells her that this is no chastisement, only a gentle ribbing.

Sonja raises her eyebrows in surprise. "Bryce, I'm disappointed in you. Did you not recognize the planet?"

My skin replays an image of the planet at its closest approach, and then overlays that with the world where Sonja and I had last been together. Of course they are the same, changes in geology notwithstanding. "Subtle."

"*I* didn't think so. I did it as a last salute," she says. "You meant a lot to me, and I needed you to know."

I squeeze her hand. "You know that your being here tells me that. I was beginning to feel that I would be doing this alone."

She wraps me in a warm hug. "Not at all," she whispers into my ear. "The time has come, and what better way to do it than with the one you love?"

Next fold is coming right now, says my skin. We both look up, and watch as the red star slides into view directly overhead. *The last fold will be a while.*

"May we join you?" comes a voice.

I look at Sonja in surprise. She's smiling. "Who is that?" I ask.

"It's Simon, Bryce. We're all up here, and have been waiting patiently for you to arrive."

This information is more than I can digest. "*All* of you?" I sit down on the cool grass.

"All of us. If you'll have us, that will make this a party of eight."

"Please. Come down, come down."

"We've been talking about it for some time now," says Sonja. "They told me just a decade ago that they were prepared to come along. But they were all rather firm that they wanted it to be a surprise."

Soon enough Sonja and I are watching Simon's tall and slender silver spaceship land on the parking lot across the street. Our skins are up and over our faces to protect us from the ferocious glare of the rockets—Simon has always been very traditional in his ways—and to keep the radiation down until it can be reduced to an acceptable level.

Once the smoke has blown away, a door opens up high above the sharp fins and an elegant wooden stairway descends in tight curls to the pavement. Four women and two men step out and start down the stairs, all of them waving excitedly.

Simon, Wes, Antonia, Marie, Dawn and Bonnie. There are hugs and kisses all around, and then we stand and just look at one another for several minutes. It takes a long time for our drones to come up with the appropriate memories, but we all agree that the last time we were all together was when the Stewardship and Extinction Committee was struck.

Something like seven billion years ago.

We are sitting together around the kitchen table, our supper finished and now a nice glass of wine for each of us, courtesy of a stock that Simon has kept on his spaceship for such an occasion. For the moment we are all content to just sit back and enjoy the feeling, and, likely, to use the silence as an excuse to recall how to behave when others are around.

"I had trouble believing you when you said you had found Earth," says Dawn, finally breaking the silence.

"I think we all did," says Antonia. "I thought it was lost forever."

"The Sentinel did an excellent job of covering its tracks," replies Bonnie. "With Jupiter and Saturn collapsed in on each other and flung through the fold it had constructed, I think we all figured Earth had gone with them."

"I was certainly fooled," says Wes. "When the fold opened up over New Home and the gas giant complex fell through, my first thought was to rush back to the home system." He shrugs. "With Earth not here, I just assumed it had gone through as well. I have a memory of leaving the carnage behind and moving on to another galaxy." He takes a sip of wine. "I guess I'd given up."

"There were three of us assigned to try and determine what went wrong," I remind them. "I can't recall who the other two were, but I'm sure it wasn't any of you." They are all silent, affirming my belief. "I was the last to get there, and the last to leave. Aside from the many sightseers who had to come and view that end of the disaster." I grin at the memory, one that is still not too hazy. "I don't ever recall seeing so many different races in one system before, and they all wanted to ask me questions, to take up pieces of my time."

I pause for a sip of wine. "But I think it was because I was there longer that I happened across the secondary fold, and I realized that maybe the Sentinel had sent Earth on a different path. From there it was just a matter of some fairly basic math and physics to determine where it was going, although the extra folds that the Sentinel had thrown in its path did make the job a little harder."

Sonja rubs the back of my neck. "You did well, Bryce. There are only so many true memories left. The Earth should rightfully be a part of them."

"Both first and last," I say. I wipe a slight tear from my eye.

Ladies and gentlemen, says my skin, as the other skins are saying to their wearers, *if you will come outside now, the last fold is about to occur.*

We all rise and top up our glasses, and then file out the front door to stand on the lawn. We tilt our gazes up and look at the distant red star.

The final moments are upon us.

My last visit to Earth occurred many billions of years ago, shortly after the Stewardship and Extinction Committee had first met. The sun had brightened by then, superheating the atmosphere and boiling away all of the planet's oceans. By then all life had already left the planet, but as a nod to our heritage, we had placed a Sentinel overhead to guard and to care for our ancestral home.

Before that, somewhere there was a memory of sitting on a beach, enjoying a warm yellow sun and cool water, and watching girls in swimsuits walk by. I must have been in my teens then.

We go through the fold, and find ourselves standing on a dead planet that is falling towards the photosphere of a Red Giant. Sol, our sun, more than one hundred and sixty six times its original size. It has already swallowed Mercury and Venus. We are here to give it the gift of Earth, to restore as much of our sense of the natural order to our home system as we can.

The planet is rushing through space now, the sun a giant red ball that covers almost the entire sky. Our skins rise up to cover our faces again, and I nervously take a quick sip of wine, the skin allowing it to slide between my lips.

For a moment this is more difficult than I had imagined it would be. The urge to continue is obviously a strong one, built into me, and into all of us, through genetics and history. I close my eyes for a second, and then open them and look around me. Everyone else seems to feel the same, but resolution is something that we all seek now, and with the Committee no longer required, the exhaustion of such a long life is beginning to filter in. There can only be the one resolution.

Your memory drones safely ejected from orbit after the last fold, announces my skin. *They will continue to receive from you as long as they can. If there is anyone left in the galaxy, or for that matter the universe, that wishes to learn something from them, they should remain viable until the very end.*

We all smile and nod our heads. I reach over and hug Sonja, and then we are all holding each other, first in tight enfolding hugs, and then arm in arm as we continue to watch the sky. There may be a small touch of fear, but this is right. For we are tired after so very long, and now it is time to rest.

My first published story, this one was also derived from a sleep-induced vision, me riding a recumbent tricycle through the desert, held up by several colorful helium balloons so that I remained about a foot above the ground. Follow the dots from that initial moment of psychedelia and I'm sure you can easily see how I got to my end point.

FATHER TIME

The bar I'm in is quiet. Three in the afternoon, not many people here. Two young men play darts against the far wall, and a middle-aged couple sit at a table with drinks. She smokes, he doesn't.

My waitress smiles sympathetically at me, knowing instinctively that something is wrong, but not sure what it is. I try to muster up a grin for her, but by the look on her face I'd say I've only managed to frighten her. She leaves my gin and orange on the table and walks away quickly.

I nurse the drink for a while, thinking about as little as I can. Too much thinking drags my mind back to the hospital; not a place I want it to be right now.

When my drink is about half-empty the outside door swings open and someone walks in, silhouetted against the bright sunlight. I squint for a moment, then turn my face away from the door.

So I hear, rather than see, the man come up to my table. I turn to tell him that I am not interested in company right now, but what I see stops me short.

The man, I realize, is my father. I am startled and it must show on my face. He smiles, and there are none of the lines that I know so well, the lines that have invaded his face with age.

I know this for a fact. I watched him as I grew, watched as he fought the losing Battle of Vanity. As the face that had once seemed so effortlessly smooth, so wonderful as a child in awe to stroke in wonder, slowly gave ground to the rifts and valleys of living.

This is my father as he was when he was a young man. But I just came from visiting my father in the hospital, where he is now losing an even more important battle.

The man who was my father steps up to me, and I reach out to stroke his face.

He lets me touch his skin for a second, and then says, "Let's go somewhere else and talk."

"This is my fifth trip," he says, after taking a sip of coffee. We are in The Silk Hat, in a booth near the back. He used to come in here and have his tea leaves read, but not today. What would tea leaves say about a man whose only reason for existence is an apparent quirk in the mathematics of the universe?

I watch the waitress as she goes by, uncomfortable talking while others are nearby. She goes to the only other occupied booth, near the door. We are near the back of the restaurant.

"Where do you go next?" I ask. It is hard for me to accept this, although not for the reasons you might think. Rather than being freaked by his being here, I am most bothered by the fact that he is appearing here younger than me.

"Ten more years. Each step takes me further away, but it seems to get easier."

"How . . . " I begin.

"Do I do it?" He shakes his head. "I can't explain. Even if I could, it would sound like a lot of spiritual mumbo-jumbo to you. What do people now call it? Sort of new age."

"Oh. You mean like mantras and crystals and stuff?"

"No." That's all he says.

I decide to change topics, although I realize as I speak I could have done better. "You realize you're dying."

He grimaces, and I see the first hints of those lines. "With?"

"Cancer. All through the body. Probably only days left." Tears start, I grab a napkin and try to staunch the flow.

He takes my hand and grieves with me. For himself.

I grieve for lost time.

The next day, he dies. I am downstairs having a cup of tea and thinking about my childhood, and I feel a hand on my shoulder. It is the nurse; she has tears in her eyes. My father has been very popular here.

I stand too suddenly, knocking the cup to the floor. The tea that is left spills in slow motion, and when it hits the floor it spreads in every direction. I feel the eyes of many people on my back, but those looks, whether judgmental or sympathetic, only touch me for the shortest of moments.

The nurse hugs me, briefly, then leads me to the elevator like I'm a little boy. Which is what I am right now, remembering stroking the smooth skin only yesterday, and then seeing the parched and sagging folds of his face today.

It was too much, and I had to leave. So I missed the moment of his death. We get off the elevator and the nurse takes me to the room and then leaves, shutting the door behind her.

His fault; he could have come to me after he died. As I look at the body one last time I punch the wall in fury and slide sobbing to the floor.

"I missed it," says a voice.

I look up, and there is my father. Only older than yesterday, by about ten years.

I don't talk to him, but rather I fold my arms and sulk. He's abandoned me, I hate him.

"I need your help. Please."

"Why?"

"I'm stuck. There's been a war, I can't leave this future. The fabric has changed."

"Then how are you here?"

"This isn't me, or at least not the me you saw yesterday. But this is the reason I will die, or did die, of cancer."

"I don't understand."

A flash of anger in his eyes. "You don't need to understand. Just meet me at the head of the Mill Creek Trail at twelve noon, ten years from today. And bring a good calculator, a good HP scientific."

"If there's a war, how do you know I will be alive to be there?"

"You've already been there. That's why I'm able to be here."

"And if I don't show?"

"Then I die there, and not here." He gestures at the bed, and his body is no longer there. Then he disappears and is replaced with the diseased version of himself. Fading in and out of my vision. "You can't bury me," coughs, "this way, son."

"Fuck. Fine."

The old one goes to the bed and lies down, closes his eyes and stops breathing. The other comes back. "Don't forget."

"Like you didn't forget me?"

I now see pain in his eyes. That cut deep, and I can see him start to retort, catch himself, hold it back. "Ten years. Please."

He goes away again. Too much. My father has left me four times in two days.

Everything around me loses focus, and the tubes and machines seem to become a beast that has come to suck the life force from my father's silent body. I howl in anguish, and two nurses rush in. One quietly holds my elbow while the other takes the dangling tubes from my hand. I realize I have ripped them from his body.

The tears flow again, far more than any time before.

He was right about the war. Canada and the States take lots of refugees now, but only from Europe. The population of my city has swollen into the millions, food is harder to get, almost no one travels by car.

They say it is still a democracy; I think it is a police state. Curfews, elections that don't matter, soldiers on every street corner. But we are still alive.

The appointed day has come. The calculator I bought four years ago, before such luxuries disappeared forever. I also bring a bottle of wine, hoping to share it with my father. Over the course of these hard years I have forgiven him his sins against me.

I'm early, so I sit on an old bench and wait. The park I am in is still green, after a fashion. The path is paved, but aspen, bushes and weeds choke the sides, and every so often there is a spruce. Different foliage from when I was a child, but they are all that will grow here now.

Some people say the parkland is a luxury, but it is one thing our leaders have not budged on. We were once famous for our green space, and I think the doddering old timers who now run our lives remember those days with affection.

Two soldiers walk by, eyeing me warily. But their rifles stay down, and they continue their patrol without stopping to question me. I see one whisper something to the other and they both laugh, casting a parting glance my way.

Finally, after perhaps a half hour he steps out of some bushes.

"Father."

He looks startled. "Why are you here?"

I offer him the calculator. "You came to me, said you were stuck here because of the war."

"War?"

I nod. "Nuclear, in the Middle East."

He turns the calculator on, does some quick calculations. "Can I have this?"

I nod. He puts it in his coat pocket.

I offer him the bottle of wine, intending to suggest we share it. He takes it, looks at it, says "Thanks," and disappears.

I stand at the trail head, dismayed. "Father!" I shout, "Don't leave me again!"

But he's gone.

"There was no war."

"What do you mean?" I have introduced this man to the nurse as my nephew. He is fresh-faced at nineteen, still two years away from becoming a father.

"I mean that you remember it because of your connection with me, but it didn't happen."

"How?" The medication adds to my perplexity.

"I changed the equations. Had to."

"Why?"

"I wouldn't be able to travel, otherwise. No one around you remembers it. It faded away for good, and was replaced by other emergencies and tragedies."

"But what about my life? Where did everything go?"

"Still the same. Only, people have begun to find different reasons for the choices that have been made over the years."

This is a sobering thought. Even with the evidence of my father's travels, I had thought certain things were immutable. Was I so drastically wrong?

"What does this do to my work?"

"Nothing. Everything else stays the same. The changes I am able to make are very localized, and take much subjective, objective, and imaginary time to occur. And this is the only one I have ever made that affected more people than myself."

I try to think of more questions, but the meds in my system are making this all very hard to grasp. At least, I think it's the drugs.

He takes the opportunity afforded by the silence to open his shoulder bag and pulls out two crystal glasses and a familiar-looking bottle of wine. He pours the wine, rests the glasses on the bed table. "Here. Let me help you sit up."

Tubes get in the way, but he helps me up. For a moment my bedroom spins around, but it settles down soon enough. When I found I was ill I insisted on home nursing, rather than an impersonal hospital.

The insurance company had balked, but I have spent my years wisely, cultivating friendships with many who now lead this newly independent northern land. A word from one of them, and my apartment was readied for my dying. It makes it easier to turn away visitors, too, but the young man here today is special.

He puts a straw in my glass, holds it for me to take a sip. "Mmm. Very good. How old is it?"

He thinks for a second. "Can't really say. Somewhere between five years and two hundred, I think."

I remember the wine now. Tears come to my eyes. "I'm glad you came back."

I stretch out my hand and stroke his face. The look of my weathered hand on his skin is jarring, and I remember where I am.

"Join me," he says.

I cough, spitting some of the wine back up. He holds a cloth napkin to my mouth, and it comes away pink, even though the wine is white. The nurse looks in, sternly. "How?" I ask.

"It's easy," he replies. "Just lie down and close your eyes. I'll go get you elsewhen."

The tears rush back. The joy I feel is almost painful. My father wants me with him! After so many years that I thought he wanted to be away from me.

He's crying, too. "I missed you, son. I wasn't a very good dad."

"It's okay. I spent a long time being angry with you, but I think I finally came to my own reconciliation."

"Is all this why you never had a family?"

A good question. I gesture for him to help me lie back down while I think on it. He seems content to let me be quiet as I think, and I hear no sounds of impatience from him. Eventually I say, "Probably. You're very wise for someone who only looks nineteen.

This makes him laugh; a boisterous sound that brings back a flood of visions. Tears well up in my eyes again. At least the lousy disease hasn't dried me out.

"You know I'm not really nineteen."

I nod. I spent much of my life trying to understand the physics involved, even going so far as to go back to university and getting a doctorate. One of few that the government still allows complete studies in.

My work did much for me, and I hope it did much for the world at large. And I became important enough that people began to listen to me, and with my help some libertarians started to find their way into public office again. Perhaps my contributions will eventually make it easier for personal freedoms to become important again.

But I never could figure out how my father avoided the conventional pitfalls of paradox, as well as the unconventional ones that dogged my work for so many years. Maybe now I can find out.

"Where will we go?"

He smiles. "You name it. The universe will be ours."

I smile in return, and hope my toothless grin doesn't scare him away. "It's a deal."

Then I close my eyes and slip away.

I am nineteen, and I have a small backpack packed, but I don't know why. My father comes into the room. "Son, I have someone I'd like you to meet."

Then my father walks into the room, only he's young, younger than I ever knew as a child. He stands beside the father I know, the father who after my mother died always spent so much time away from me, and suddenly I remember!

I remember it all, the meetings, my father's death, the war. Even my own death. A wave of relief washes over me, as I realize that I am being given a new chance to discover my father and my relationship with him.

"You ready?"

I nod so hard I give myself a headache. "Yes!"

They both hug me, something I'm not used to from my father, then they hug each other.

My older father holds my shoulders for a minute, staring into my eyes. "You be careful son, but enjoy yourself."

All of this affection stuns me. "I wish you could come too."

Both of them laugh. "I already have," he says, "and I already am."

I still don't understand, but perhaps with time, as it were, I will.

"Where are we going?" I ask.

"We'll go say goodbye to yourself first. Then . . . " He shrugs his shoulders.

I smile and we go. I wonder where else I've already been.

Some stories just bubble up from somewhere well-hidden even to the author. I do know I had read an excellent article in Outside *magazine on an older gentleman who lived somewhere in the Caribbean and still hunted the odd whale from a rather small boat, but I'm pretty sure that was stumbled upon only after I had finished the first draft.*

DAY'S HUNT

They broke out of the foam just after sunrise. The sun hung low on the horizon, fat and bloated and rust-colored, streaks of rusty orange streaming out of it, leaking into the shit-brown air.

The steady *sshh* of the brown and yellow foam rubbing against the ancient hull was replaced, intermittently at first, and then with a constant display, by the thumps and scrapes and rubbings of the topmost layer of the landfill sea. Davies, searching the horizon for their prey, leaned over the side and watched for a moment as the refuse of centuries bumped and bobbed to the surface.

The ship, *Ew York Tim*, fought its way through the mixture of liquid and solid with a special engine built hundreds of years before Davies' time, and kept running with scavenged parts dredged up from the depths or cobbled from other such vessels after they had finally been committed to the dumps. Admiral Yates was especially talented at finding and magically recycling, and Kelly, his engineer, had a knack for keeping the worst-sounding junker running another day.

The others were coming out on deck now. The Admiral and Smythe were joined by Jimbo, Kelly, Rohan, Domingo, and Archambault. Blackie climbed up the ladder to the nest, Martins came forward to stand with Davies.

The Admiral stood on the top deck, held an ancient brass spyglass to his right eye, the metal battered and burnished with age. So far the horizon yielded nothing of import, so Davies turned his attention back to the Admiral, who would most likely be quicker to spot any action.

The Admiral's cap feather ruffled slightly in the breeze, and his pigeon, Heinz, danced anxiously on his right shoulder, nervous at the cries of the gulls as they awoke and launched themselves towards the ship, hoping for scraps of whatever. Spots of white marched a line down the front and back of the Admiral's coat, joined now by two more as Heinz shat up his discontent.

Davies watched the Admiral's lips move as he talked to Jimbo, the chief harpoonist, but he could hear nothing over the noisy cries of the gulls. Jimbo, a good head taller than the Admiral, leaned over and spoke directly into the old man's ear in response, compensating for a partial deafness that was the result of the Tip Wars twenty years earlier.

Martins sauntered up to where Davies was standing. This was only his second trip out, a young guy with all his teeth still and no tumors, and for some unfathomable reason he had taken to Davies. "Think we'll find any today?" They'd had no luck on Martins' first trip and had settled with scavenging from a small *Ford* that they had dredged up from below the surface.

Davies shrugged. "Don't know. They don't always come this close to the foam. But still . . ." He spread his arms wide.

Martins grunted in assent, then stiffened as the Admiral shouted "Ho!"

They turned to see where he was looking, staring hard in that direction. At first they saw nothing. But then, a spout. And then another! Two made for a very lucky sign, and they were only a few minutes away.

The Admiral came charging down to the deck, Jimbo close at his heels. His face was flushed with excitement, even under the heavy layer of screen. The others ran up and the nine of them gathered round while the Admiral laid out the plan of action.

"Jimbo. You and Archambault and Blackie head to just north of where we saw the spouts." He paused to spit up some bloody phlegm on his sleeve, stared at it for a second, and then wiped it on his pants leg, grinning wildly as he did so. Heinz danced and cooed nervously before settling back down. "The rest of you lads, split into your two teams and circle around. Drop no more than three charges each to force them up and back towards Jimbo. By *Saran,* we'll have them for sure!

There was a chorus of "Aye, sirs" and then the men jumped to action. Davies and Kelly and Domingo lowered their dory overboard, then jumped into it and started circling to the west.

The other two rowed while Davies stood and watched for signs. The dory rode relatively smoothly, pitches so small that Davies barely had to flex his knees. He kept one foot on the cleat, leaning forward and sometimes resting a hand on the bow.

The little scavenged motor at the stern whined softly, keeping the dory just a hair's-breadth above the actual surface, by what magic of technology Davies and his mates did not understand. But, more likely centuries later and unlike so many other found items it still worked, and made it easier for them all to do their jobs.

"See anything?" asked Domingo, straining at the oars.

Davies shook his head. "Just the other boats." It was impossible to see beneath the surface, so he watched the horizon for signs of breaching.

And then, there it was! A big one, maybe a tonne or more, jumping out of a large swell almost due south of them. It flew into the air with an awesome, deep-throated groan, jaws wide open and forearms flailing, and managed to catch five unsuspecting gulls; one for each three-fingered hand and three for its mouth. Then it crashed back down and quickly burrowed under the swell.

Garbage and putrid liquid flew everywhere. Oil and shit and plastic of all types for the most part, but also scrap metal that had yet to be salvaged and ancient food that was being exposed to air for the first time in centuries as the whale half burrowed and half swam to try to get down to its safe level.

Davies reached into his pouch and grabbed one of the precious charges and wound it using the key he had attached to a frayed cord tied on his wrist, then dropped it onto the surface. It immediately malfunctioned, skittering around in circles along the surface.

Domingo slapped it with an oar and it buzzed along the surface until it was almost thirty meters away. He went back to rowing as it continued to swim frantic little circles off in the distance. More and more charges failed to work nowadays, and then there was nothing to replace them.

Davies quickly wound another and tossed it over the side. This one burrowed down as it was supposed to, liquid and paper and plastics flying up like a crazed trail of exhaust. He decided to hang on to the third in case he didn't need to use it.

There were two muffled explosions as charges from the other dories went off, making a sort of double WHUMPF sound, and more trash sailed into the air. Gulls wheeled about, shrieking madly as they grabbed at bits of food that had been flung into the sky. Davies saw one gull try to fly, but its left wing had been shredded by the force of the charges. The other gulls soon noticed and attacked it mercilessly.

The two charges he had dropped went off a few seconds later. The one that had managed to burrow was drowned out by the one still on the surface. A loud bang and a gout of flame, and garbage rained down on the three of them. Davies picked a green rind of something off his shoulder, sniffed at it, then took a bite. Not too bad, so he finished it.

A great crater lay where the charge had been just a moment before, slowly filling in as the refuse about it seeped back in to fill the gap, and this time several gulls were badly injured and flopping about or already dead. Opportunistic gulls and more garbage fell from the sky, and Davies could smell some of the rotten stench the charge had kicked up.

A shout from Kelly brought his attention back to the matter at hand. They watched as the surface surged in two places, no more than five meters away. Davies quickly wound another charge, giving it two extra turns so it would go a bit deeper, and Kelly dropped his oars and hefted his harpoon. The two whales broke through, heading in just the direction the men wanted. Then Jimbo dropped a charge from his boat, and Domingo strained to bring them closer.

The whales tried to go under again, but the charge did its job and there was an explosion from deep below. Both came up quickly, obviously tired from the exertion and terrified by everything that was happening.

The big male's eyes were rolling back into his head, and Davies could see blood streaming from his nose hump and from under his right forearm. The female, perhaps a quarter-tonne lighter, had hit the surface badly after her second breach, and was obviously favoring her flukes.

Both dories swung around, Jimbo's pulling up beside the male. Blackie leaned out and grunted fiercely as he threw all of his body into his harpooning, stuck the male just before wood went to blackskin.

But the male found the strength to go under again, pulling the line from the tub and around the loggerhead, there to keep the line from playing out. "Sounding!" yelled Blackie, but Archambault, careless for a second, shrieked in pain as the speeding rope flicked sideways and ripped off his little finger, cauterizing as fast as it was torn off.

Then the rope went slack. They all looked at one another, ignoring for now the female still struggling on the surface nearby. "Be ready!" yelled Jimbo.

The big male resurfaced, a great leap that upended the dory carrying Martins, Rohan and Smythe. The flukes came up and Davies watched in horror as they snapped across the bow, barnacles attached to it acting as a serrated knife, ripping Smythe's head from his body. The head bounced across the surface, came to a stuttering stop just in front of Davies. Smythe's face held a look of surprise, maybe fear, with a hint that agony was following close behind. Davies felt his gorge rise.

And then the male turned and tried to run at them. Davies blinked back his horror, wound the last charge two short turns, and tossed it, catching the male close and possibly bursting its eardrums. It moaned, high-pitched agony, and turned back to join the female.

Domingo took the opportunity steer the dory over to Martins and Rohan, who were floundering and gasping, trying not to be sucked under by all the crap. They hauled them aboard; Rohan's leg was broken, white bone sticking out from his thigh, and one of the tumors on his neck had been ripped half off, dangling like a loose tooth. Martins was cut on his forehead, blood running so profusely he could barely see.

Everyone on board and relatively safe, they looked to the whales. It seemed that neither could even try to go under, and now the two of them were crawling along at a terribly slow pace, whimpering softly as they moved, not designed to stay for long on the surface but too weak to burrow back down to safety. Gulls shrieked mad cries and dove in to rend bits of flesh from the defenseless whales, and blood streamed down their bodies, pooling on the surface. Behind the dories the same relentless ritual was being performed on the head and body of Smythe.

Blackie steered their dory and put wood to blackskin, bumped up against the male. Jimbo took the light lance and jumped onto the whale's back, wrapped his legs around the harpoon standing like a flagpole on the whale, and began to plunge the lance. The rounded head of the lance was designed not to catch inside the whale, and so Jimbo stabbed and stabbed and stabbed, looking for the heart.

And then he found it. The whale finally stopped thrashing; a giant bubble of dark blood welled up from the blowhole and ran down its body. Its arms went limp.

The female squealed pathetically and made one last attempt to dig down, but Domingo rowed the dory in tight and Kelly drove his harpoon into her back, then lanced her from the boat, not crazy to straddle her as Jimbo had the male.

Both whales now dead, Blackie and Davies quickly tied themselves to their dories, then jumped overboard and harpooned the heads and tied the mouths closed, to keep them from shipping liquids and maybe sinking before they got back to the ship. It was an effort in the quagmire of crap and oil, but they managed, and then they roped the two around their flukes and climbed back aboard and then all the men dug in to row them back to the ship, even Martins and Rohan.

The Admiral was there to pat each man on the back as he boarded, telling them all that they'd done an excellent job, to commiserate about the death of Smythe, and to give calm orders regarding the treatment of all the injuries. All proof to the men that he was a good Admiral.

Once the whales had been hauled aboard, they were flensed and the bible leaves were cut. It was hot, sweaty, sticky work. Flies buzzed about like tiny demons, angry gulls shat on them, and the sun, now high in the sky, burned down on them, almost yellow. Hats came out for this business.

Many whalers waited until they got back to the pods floating in the foam, but the Admiral often liked to remind the men that it was best to get things done as soon as possible. And besides, he pointed out, they had eaten practically nothing but preserved garbage for the past four days, dredged up from the bottom on their last trip out.

After a short service for Smythe, it made for a big party that evening, livers and tongues roasted over a methane flame, and then music and dancing and bawdy stories. The night was filled with laughter.

The rest they preserved for the factories that floated near the pods, out there on the water that was as flat and as still as far as the eye could see, frothy and yellow.

And they would hunt some more, and hope they would have luck so close to home the next time.

I probably shouldn't admit it, but this one came with the title first; the story had to follow. And then I made the mistake of telling some people, which was followed for years by questions that all equated to "Have you written the story yet?" It's hard enough to fend off those voices when they come from inside your head, but when the bombardment is quadrophonic (as it was on at least two occasions), a man could go mad if he didn't produce something just to shut down the interrogation.

WASPS AT THE SPEED OF SOUND

Abe sat in the van for several long moments after it had stopped, breathing slowly and deeply as he eyed the copse of trees about fifty yards away, farm house and barn sitting a little ways behind. Through the slit in the windshield he could see there were signs of movement, but being this close meant he should be safe from taking a hole. The only other concern today was the fact that there were more around than ever before, and they still didn't have a clue as to why. Hopefully he wouldn't run into problems with anything new.

"Well?" came a distant voice.

Abe spun awkwardly, stared at Ryan through the scratched and pitted plastic and steel mesh. His suit squeaked as he shifted his position to get a better look. "Well what?"

Ryan cocked his head in the direction of the nest. "Well you gonna do it. You know what I mean. Your turn."

Abe sighed, his hot breath momentarily fogging up the faceplate. "Yeah. Curtain yourself. I'm opening up the door."

Ryan pulled the metal curtain across the interior of the van, latched it and sealed it. "Done!" he yelled, voice even more muffled now.

Abe popped open the back doors, shuffled his butt to the edge and gingerly stepped to the ground. The suit groaned and protested as it settled into place, haphazard-looking rivets and redone welds holding everything together. Once standing, he checked the buckle on the home-made flame thrower and then made sure everything was ready to fire.

He couldn't hear much beyond his own breathing, but as he slowly shuffled towards the trees and the nest he knew that there would be only one sound outside today. There would be no bird songs, no distant cars, no airplanes flying overhead. In the distance, across the brown and wasted wheat fields, he could see a lone combine sitting. Probably Old Vic's—the old guy himself likely sitting in the combine right now, bones bleaching in the morning sun of Indian Summer—if he had his directions right. He hated sitting in the back, not driving; besides having the easy job, driving aimlessly and looking for the signs of infestation was the closest thing he could remember to pleasant Sunday drives.

Just a few more paces and he would be at the edge of the trees. Sweat dripping down his back was making him hot and itchy, but scratching would be a luxury that would have to wait. He blinked away more perspiration from his eyes, looked down through foggy plastic at his sheet metal leggings, and then entered the little patch of woods.

The hum could be heard now, distant but growing with each step. Around him the trees were in shambles, leaves lying on the ground, randomly tattered and stripped, shredded bark hanging like dreadlocks, like the hair on the floor of a barber's shop. He saw bones on the ground, probably a rabbit, and a few more paces brought him to the skeleton of a dog. That would likely be Old Vic's shepherd, Rufus. The top of its skull was blown right off, little bits of bone lying in a spray pattern leading to the left.

The hum was much louder now, turning into a persistent, angry buzz that was already beginning to rattle his teeth. Abe heard a few distant pings as some of them ran into his suit, getting up speed for whatever journeys they were taking, forays for food or else for a web jump to wherever the hell it was that they went.

There it was. A giant gray mass of paper and puke, crawling up the trunk of a giant elm and enclosing the first three levels of branches. And everywhere there were wasps, yellowjackets by the tens of thousands, maybe even by the millions for all he knew.

More started to impact against his suit, unable to get up the speed needed to dent or break it, but enough to get Abe moving. If he waited too long they would plug up the flame thrower, and then he'd be staggering out there weighed down by more wasps than he would be able to handle, he was sure.

He turned up the flame a little, fried a few that came too close, continued to approach the nest. Five yards away he cranked it up and kept moving in, waving the stream of fire all over the nest, spreading it up the elm and making sure it jumped to the next trees as well, like a giant gray marshmallow left in the bonfire too long. Angry buzzing continued, rising to the level of a horror movie's digital soundtrack, as wasps swarmed out of the nest in one enormous black and yellow mass, trying to attack him, looking to sting him in their fury and working to weigh him down with their staggering quantity, but he was able to burn most in midair. Hundreds climbed across his faceplate, trying to get in, thrusting their stingers in futile attempts to defend the nest, but regular sweeps of his free gloved hand wiped them off, although the faceplate was pretty much useless now, smeared with yellow and green whorls of wasp guts.

It was getting too hot inside his tin suit now, so after one last gush of orange flame Abe turned and started lumbering back towards the van. Behind him the fire continued, spreading from one tree to the next and along the forest floor as well. By the time Abe had reached the van, smoke was beginning to rise from trees right beside Old Vic's house.

Abe stood there for a moment, watching as the smoke turned to actual flame, as the fire licked up the walls and along the roof and jumped across the yard to the sheds, and from there quickly to the barn, probably doing in some spiders and webs, even. Teach those fucking wasps to learn to break the sound barrier in *his* county, it would.

Ryan started the van, and it coughed billowing clouds of blue smoke in Abe's face as he wrenched open the door and sat on the floor. Two aerosol cans, one mounted on each side and primed by his leaving the van before, automatically emptied bug spray onto his suit as he inched himself backwards, then swung his legs inside and leaned on one elbow, reaching over to pull the door shut. When it was closed the spray stopped and he slammed his palm on the floor, twice. The van grunted into motion, and Abe slid the flame thrower off his shoulders and lay down on his back, letting himself rest until the ride was over. Made no sense to try to get out of this tin suit while they were moving.

The drive took about twenty-five minutes, twice as long as it used to take. But they were careful about potholes and the like, what with spare parts pretty much impossible to get nowadays. And with only one suit, if they had an accident, one of them would be stuck behind and possibly at the mercy of the bugs.

Abe felt the change in the road as they swung into their driveway, except instead of carrying on up the fifty yards of gravel, the van stopped and he heard a muffled "Jesus Christ!" from Ryan.

Abe sat up from where he was leaning, worked at the seals on his helmet for a moment and then tugged it off. "What?" The tangy chemical smell of bug spray made his eyes tear up.

"There's a car in the driveway, parked in front of the garage."

"Son of a bitch!" Abe awkwardly got to his knees and crawled up front, slid the metal curtain back to the side and looked. Sure enough, there was a green Taurus sedan sitting in front of the garage door, its driver's side door hanging open. "Think we can sneak around it, get the garage open?"

Ryan shook his head. "Too close. The door would hit it when it swung up." He turned and looked at Abe. "You've got the suit on. Looks like you get to go out there and see if you can find the driver or else move it yourself."

Abe grimaced, then slid back to get the helmet, put it on. Ryan shut the curtain again, and then Abe slid out and closed the van doors behind him. This time he left the flame thrower in the van, figuring the bulk of it would just get in his way.

Not many people out on the roads these days, and there sure as hell weren't many stupid enough to drive unprotected in something like this Taurus. There were fewer nests than there were six months ago, Abe knew from the dish out back that picked up the new CNN headquarters in Antarctica, every Saturday when they fired up the generator for two hours. But there were still plenty of them, and that didn't even factor in the ants and beetles and bees and roaches and every other fucking insect on the planet. Thank God all the little critters that lived on people's bodies seemed to have jumped ship first thing; he'd read about one bug that lived at the base of your eyelashes, and he still had nightmares about the endless possibilities with *that* one.

He heard a faint beeping sound as he approached the car, wasn't surprised to look in through the shattered driver's side window and see that the keys were still in place. Maybe he could start it up and shift it into reverse without climbing in, as if he could ever fit wearing this home-made armor. Abe reached in to try just that when he heard another sound, a distant moan. He stepped back and walked around the open door, heard the sound again.

Shit.

There was a man lying face down on the ground, bloody gouge about three inches long on his left shoulder. So far there were no bugs on him; he must have got here just before they did, got smacked by a wasp or a bee as he was trying to run from the car to the house.

Nothing else to do about it. Abe leaned over and flipped him onto his back and grabbed the guy's ankles, started dragging him along the ground towards the kitchen porch. They had a door there, he would be safe from most bugs for at least a few minutes.

The man moaned again, louder this time, then opened his eyes and looked at Abe, dark eyes panicky with fear.

"It's okay," Abe shouted. "I'm trying to help you. Do you think you can stand up?"

The man nodded, so Abe slowly kneeled down and held out an arm, let the man take it and helped as he pulled himself up to a sitting position, then after a very brief rest up to standing. The man leaned on him then as they shuffled the last few feet to the door. Abe opened it and then pushed the man in, watched him stumble to a kneeling position. "Stay there," he yelled, hoping the guy would understand his muffled voice through all of his obvious pain. "Don't open any doors. We'll come and get you in a few minutes."

Abe then shut the door, shuffled back to the Taurus and thought for a second about how he could do this. No way in hell he was going to take the suit off; likely as not after his little search and destroy mission there were still a lot of pissed-off wasps in the area, maybe working up a good head of steam. He finally settled on leaning his faceplate against the door jam along the roof, leaned in so that his arm reached past over the top of the steering wheel. It took some doing, but he managed to bend his wrist enough to turn the key, and after a few missed attempts he held it long enough for the car to fire up.

He gave a thumbs-up to Ryan back in the van, then turned the steering wheel so the car would slide off the driveway and out of the way. Then he grabbed a two by four that was lying beside the garage, used it to depress the brake, then slipped it into gear and pushed himself off the car, falling to his back and watching as the open driver's side door scraped over his booted toes. But the car did what it was supposed to do, speeding up as it tipped into the ditch, then coming to a squishy halt as it crunched into the drying mud. To keep any mosquitoes from breeding they'd emptied the water from the ditch weeks ago, and so even though the car sat at precarious position, it was likely still salvageable.

The garage door opened, powered by dedicated solar cells on the roof that were installed by Ryan before it got too dangerous to be out and unprotected. Aside from chasing down nests to burn, all of Ryan's free time went into building more cells and scheming how to install them without getting hurt or killed. The van drove past as Abe rolled over and slowly pulled himself to his knees, and the door closed behind him as he walked in.

The van shut off now, they both stood stock still and silent, waiting for the ticking of the van's engine to stop. When it did, they listened, only moving to the next step when they felt pretty sure nothing had come in with them.

Ryan jumped out of the van and ran to grab the tank of insecticide that was hanging by the door, began to spray to replenish the four-inch wide moat made from PVC piping that had been cut in half, dropped in to replace chopped out concrete just inside the door. As Abe pulled off his helmet Ryan was already spraying the edges of the door, and then checking the battery power before switching on the two bug zappers that were still working, one hanging inside the garage and one from a tree near the front door of the house.

"You done?"

Abe slipped off the second boot, nodded as he threw the suit into the back of the van. "Yeah. Let's go find out who the fuck this guy is."

The side door opened to a hallway made of sheet metal, taken from the large amount of supplies in Ryan's welding shop that was attached to the back of the garage. It was built low, only about five feet, so they had to crouch as they made their way to the house.

The door at the other end opened into the cellar, was again surrounded by a moat of insecticide. Abe held his breath has he went over it, felt his eyes tear up again nonetheless. Down a few steps, and then they were in Ryan's cellar, walls lined with shelves, shelves lined with cans and cans of food. Ryan had always been a borderline survivalist, never quite committed to some of the extremes of the calling, overdoing it on others.

They ran upstairs and came out in the kitchen, hopped over to the door overlooking the enclosed porch. The stranger was still there, sitting against the wall by the inside door now, eyes closed but obviously breathing.

"Anything?" asked Abe.

Ryan shook his head. "Not that I can see. Let's get him in here."

He swung open the door and the two of them jumped out and grabbed the man, one on each side, then slid back through the door and closed it with a bang. Abe settled the man onto a chair and started taking off his shirt while Ryan grabbed the first-aid kit from a cupboard beside the wood stove.

Soon enough they had the man cleaned up and bandaged, and Abe had been able to get him to choke down one precious aspirin with a small glass of water. The wound wasn't too bad, although the stranger's arm would take some time to heal right. The wasp that had swiped him didn't seem to have left any venom behind, and strictly by good luck it hadn't holed him, had only left a ragged shallow tear. There was some broken glass on his clothing, but thankfully none seemed to have become imbedded in the wound.

After drinking the last of the water, the man gasped as he put the cup down on the table, said "Thanks."

"You're welcome," said Ryan. "Now who the hell are you and what are you doing here?"

"My name is Mike Perez." Pause for a breath. "I'm a rep for an electronics company, or at least I was, before all this started to happen." Another pause. "Listen," he said, looking up at the two of them. "Have you got someplace more comfortable to sit?"

Abe and Ryan looked at each other, then they nodded, Abe helping him up and leading him into the living room. Ryan sat in his big La-Z-Boy in front of the several pieces of sheet metal that used to be the picture window, Abe eased Mike into the old overstuffed chair that sat underneath the twelve-point rack and the two holes from the first wasps, and then he sat in the wooden rocker by the boarded-up fireplace.

Mike took a second to get comfortable, delicately touching his shoulder a couple of times, then he started. "I was caught up the road in Drumheller, managed to hide out with a client of mine, owner of a store. He was stocked up pretty good, but his wife was caught across town, visiting with friends. Before the phones gave out she called, told him they were running out of supplies. He left to get her . . ." Mike paused, looked at where the window used to be, like he was watching the view. "Didn't come back."

"So why did you leave?" asked Abe.

"He had a good batch of batteries, some nights I could still pick up distant stations broadcasting stuff about the bugs. I heard that the nests were getting more rare as time went on, then I heard about the webs."

Ryan and Abe both nodded.

"I figured I was safe from most other bugs in this area, as long as I stayed away from them. There aren't any ant lions, like those ones whose pits swallowed the motocross racers first days down in Arizona, and most of the other ones are pretty much no immediate threat to me, just wiping out crops and the like." He closed his eyes for a second, yawned. "I'm sorry," he said, smiling now at the two of them. "Long drive. Anyhow. I was sitting in the house one night about a week ago when I started listening to the crickets. I mean *really* listening. Have you heard them out here?"

Abe and Ryan both nodded. "For a while there they were ungodly loud," said Ryan.

"There's a rhythm to what they were chirping. I was lying on the couch in the living room late that night, listening to their sounds, wondering if it was portentous of something else . . ."

"Poor what?" interrupted Abe.

"Means like an omen," said Ryan. Abe nodded, understanding. He'd often wondered what disturbing bug shit would follow from the previous event, but knew better than to ever try to guess.

"They were speaking to me." Both Abe and Ryan stared sharply at Mike now, not sure what to think. "I was almost positive." Now he looked almost sheepish. "I remember from when I was a Boy Scout, we had to study Morse code. I listened all night, thought I could make out some words, but not all. So early the next morning I went to the library, before the sun came up but after dark."

"You went *out?* Shit, did you have any protection?"

Mike shook his head. "It was stupid, I know, but I had to know what they were saying. I thought it might be important, and besides, I knew I wasn't going too far staying in that house. Food was starting to get low."

"So did you find a book on Morse?" asked Ryan.

Mike nodded. "I did." With his good hand he pulled a small book out of a pocket and waved it at them. "A nice little pocket guide."

"And?" Neither man looked or felt particularly surprised by what they knew was coming, considering everything else the bugs had been capable of. It was just a matter of *what* they were saying.

"It was Morse. Don't ask me how they learned it. Might as well explain the wasps, or termite mounds in Africa and Australia that can be seen from space, or those mosquitoes . . ." He stared at the sheet metal again.

"Well?"

"They were saying goodbye. Telling anyone who could be bothered to listen why they were leaving, and why everything with the bugs went all to hell."

"You got all that from listening to some crickets?" asked Ryan.

Mike nodded. "I didn't get the sense that they were rubbing it in, but rather that they sort of felt, I don't know, I guess obligated to tell us. Like there were some of them that felt bad about deserting us."

Abe shook his head. "Jesus. I don't know if I should think that you're for real, or if you're just a crazy fucker who went for the world's most frightening joy ride."

Mike grinned. "Just wait, then. It gets even better."

"Do tell," said Ryan.

"According to what I was able to overhear, there's an extra-big spider web happening somewhere near here. That's the one that they're going to be using."

"Using for what?" Abe scratched at his belly; even in the cool of the mornings that they used before the bugs were really up and about, he got heat rash something fierce every time he wore the suit, and it was starting to get to him now.

"The webs are—I guess you'd call them portals, although apparently a lot of them end up being false starts, or maybe experiments to figure out where they're going. Turns out the spiders are more capable with higher math than the insects—I don't know, maybe something to do with those extra two legs. But this portal is the real deal, and the bugs are going to be using it night and day very soon."

"Yeah, we knew that they were using the webs for jumps of some sort," said Ryan. "We figured it out pretty fast. But the bugs, mostly wasps, that we've been watching usually go in and then come back out a while later. And it sure doesn't seem like there's any particular web for them. Whichever one is handy seems to do the trick."

"That's because they've been searching," said Mike. "And whatever they were looking for, they found with this newest web."

"And that web is . . ."

"Right near here, at some farm that was owned by a guy named Vic."

Ryan and Abe looked at each other. "That's where I was trying to go when the wasp hit me. Almost went into the ditch, and after I got control of the car I saw the driveway to your place, figured I'd be able to find some safety in a deserted old house and a way to patch myself up. Didn't count on passing out after I opened the door." He paused to stretch out his left arm, grimacing before letting it drop to rest on the chair again. "Anyhow, I would think that there should be other webs in other places around the world, but it sounds to me like the one around here will be used by a shitload of bugs."

"Well, hell," said Abe. "I don't recall seeing any web like that today. Maybe I missed it."

"So then maybe we should go back to Old Vic's, find this web and give it a good toasting," said Ryan.

Mike shook his head. "Nonononono." He made it sound like one word. "Don't you get it?"

Abe and Ryan looked at each other. "Get what?" asked Abe.

"Jesus, think about it. All these bugs doing these amazing new things, did we ever once have any idea why it was happening? Any real knowledge about why everything was going to hell?"

They thought for a second. Finally, Abe said, "Guess not. I think everybody just figured it was some weird-ass punishment from God, or else a virus from outer space, or some other such idiocy. But now that you mention, I never did hear anyone who sounded like they had a clue."

Mike stood up and grimaced, massaged his shoulder. "We never knew what was going on with the bugs, and we never knew what was going on inside *here* with the bugs." He tapped his temple.

Both men looked at him expectantly, and finally Mike waved his good arm in an arc. "Now we do. The way I understand it, they're going someplace better, someplace that we haven't fucked up. Mother Earth has finally decided to toss one these grenades back our way, and the bugs are the ones who get the benefit with a nice clean new place to call home." Abe made to say something, but Mike held up a finger to keep him from talking. "And those of us smart enough to figure out what's up are welcome to tag along."

Ryan shook his head. "That's the stupidest thing I ever heard of. Dumber even than you coming here in the first place. No way in hell that the bugs are gonna let us go anywhere they're planning on going, especially if they're leaving because of how fucked up things are. How do you think things got fucked up in the first place?"

Mike shrugged, then grimaced as a bolt of pain stabbed through his shoulder. "I can't say for sure why. But the messages were clear, and I do have some ideas. I figure that the web only stays open for a certain amount of time, and there can only be so many people that can make it here by then. So they sure as hell don't have to worry about overpopulation by us for anything like the immediate future."

"What about food?" asked Abe. "Crops, cows, stuff to drink. Hell, even jelly beans."

"The way I have it figured, everything we really need has to be on the other side, because everything we need the bugs need too. And if the bugs can use it, so can we. So they've either gone to some way off alien world where things are close enough to the same that they can start again, or else they've flipped through sort of like alternate Earths until they found one that matched what was here, except without the people."

"And what if you're wrong?"

Mike gave a slight smile. "Then I'm wrong. But that just means I die there instead of here. 'Cause when the bugs are all gone, things aren't going to last here. It's bad enough that some of them have gone crazy and are trying to kill us, on purpose or not, but once this world doesn't have anymore insects, it won't be long before everything else starts to fall apart. Just think how the coming winter is going to be, with the shape of the crops this year, plus the fact it'll be a bitch to get any that did survive to the markets. I figure any death here is probably going to be more painful and drawn-out."

Ryan got up out of his chair and paced around the room for a minute. The other two were quiet, Abe watching him walk and Mike rubbing his shoulder, eyes closed. Finally, Ryan stopped and fingered the two wasp holes in the wall.

Abe remembered the day they'd hit, window shattering like a bomb had hit, two solid THOCKs as the wasps had embedded themselves in the cedar paneling, and then their pointy little butts waving in the air. After realizing they weren't being shot at, Ryan had got up and tried to squash the wasps with the heel of his boot, but that had only made them angrier, and both had started to scrabble even harder, looking for purchase to pull themselves out.

So Abe had gone for the tool box and clamped a wrench over one's butt, and then with a good hard yank pulled it out of the wall. The son of a bitch had almost ripped the wrench out of his hands—had thrown him back and sent him rolling on to the floor, as a matter of fact—and the only reason it hadn't done more damage was because Ryan had dug out a hammer and wailed on it a good four or five times until it was finally still. The second wasp they'd been more ready for, and still had almost lost it when it had buzzed its wings and crazily jabbed at them and at the wrench with its stinger.

"How do other people find out?" Ryan's question interrupted Abe's reverie. "If we're gonna go through, other people will have to as well. Shit, we're sure as hell gonna need some women."

Abe laughed, a bitter sound. They'd joked about this time and again, and while no gal in a bar had ever used the "not if you're the last man on Earth" line with either of them, they had come close a few times.

Mike nodded his head. "That's the advantage of being in electronics. I have a CB radio in the car, and I was putting out word the whole way here. I figure about fifty people heard me on channel nine and responded, and most of them sounded like they were going to try and make it."

"I guess there might be people who didn't hear you but also figure out what the bugs were trying to say," Abe remarked. "Figured out the code and all."

Ryan grinned. "That'll bring us a bunch of Boy Scouts and soldiers."

"So then they can tie knots and take orders," said Abe. Everyone laughed.

Abe then excused himself and went to the kitchen and started to throw something together for supper. They did have some potatoes still sitting in the root cellar, but he decided to leave those alone for the moment and just open up a couple cans of soup. He set the little propane camp stove on the middle of the table and lit it up—gas for the stove was no longer coming through—then emptied the contents of the two cans into a pot. Mike followed him in and sat on a chair, massaging his shoulder.

"Where's Ryan?"

"Said he was going to hit the john before he ate."

"Ah." Abe stirred in silence for a few seconds. "Do you think all of the bugs are gonna go through?"

Mike pursed his lips, thinking for a few seconds. "I don't know. I can't imagine that all of them can make it here in time. I mean, there are an awful lot of them that don't fly, and the vast majority don't have the speed that the wasps and hornets have."

Abe chuckled. "Yeah. Somehow I can't imagine a butterfly coming up here from Australia or something."

"Like I said, maybe there are more portals. Maybe what I heard was just the news about one for a certain region."

The soup was bubbling. "Ryan! Soup's on!" yelled Abe.

"Coming!"

He grabbed three bowls and spoons and set them on the table, then emptied the pot into the bowls. Mike reached over and grabbed a bowl, started to eat. "Jesus," he said. "Real food. You don't know how sick I was of cereal bars and cookies."

"Enjoy then," said Ryan, coming into the kitchen. "If we really do follow them through the web, we sure as hell won't be able to carry all this shit with us."

As Mike went to take another bite there was a loud CRACK! from the living room, followed by three more in quick succession, and then a loud reverberating bang. "Shit!" He jumped and ran, followed closely by Abe and Mike.

One piece of metal that had been covering the window was now lying on the floor, and they could see from across the room that there were four huge dents in it, close to one edge. But looking around the room there were no bugs to be seen. Not that that meant anything.

"Get the stuff!" yelled Ryan. His voice was frantic with fear.

Abe dashed back through the kitchen to the workbench they kept near the back porch. Lighter, can of lighter fluid, another can of bug spray, and two hammers were always kept in a little tool box sitting right in the middle of it. He grabbed the box and ran back to the living room. Ryan and Mike were standing against one wall, both scanning the corners of the room.

"Anything?" asked Abe. He was almost out of breath, and his hands were shaking.

Ryan took the lighter and fluid, tossed the bug spray to Mike, and left Abe to take the hammer. "Nope. Which means that they're outside already, or they slipped away and managed to make it to another room, or else if they hit it at the bottom and it swung out before dropping, they're sitting underneath the metal right now."

"With our luck, third one's most likely," said Mike.

"I agree, except if they are under there they're being pretty fucking quiet," said Ryan.

"Well, what the hell was it?" asked Abe. "Couldn't be the wasps. They managed to get control of their flying almost two weeks ago. No way they'd run into a house like this by mistake anymore. They know their flight paths, know how to avoid all the big shit like us here." He stopped, mouth open, a thought forming in his mind.

"Jesus, Abe, close your mouth. You look like you're trying to catch bugs the stupid way."

He looked back at Ryan. "Sorry, man. Just occurred to me that maybe what we have here are guests. Bugs from elsewhere, coming for the web. Maybe they don't have any ideas about where it's safe to fly and where it isn't.

"So it's starting now," whispered Mike.

"Look," said Ryan. "Can we just take care of the fucking bugs in my living room first, and then start worrying about all the other shit that's going on? Please?"

Abe looked up at the open window. "Good idea. Guess we'd better do it so that we can get that thing sealed up again. Then we can figure out everything else."

"Right." Ryan took a couple of steps forward, then got down on one knee and leaned over, trying to peer underneath the metal. "Mike, you get ready with that spray. It usually doesn't kill them, but it makes them weak and dizzy enough so that they don't make a beeline for you. As soon as Abe and I lift this up, I need you to blanket everything with it."

"Then what?" he asked.

"Then I take a hammer to them, if possible," replied Abe. "If it's too hard to get in a few good whacks, then I'll hang on to the metal and Ryan will try to fry them."

"But we only want to do that as a last resort," said Ryan. "Just in case we get carried away and try to burn down the house or something." He grinned. "But this should be easier than it used to be, because now we have this third set of hands. So you ready?"

Mike lifted the can of bug spray and nodded his head. His face was calm, but both men could see the fear in his eyes. "Have to do it some time," he said, barely whispering.

Ryan and Abe each grabbed and end, and then Ryan counted off, "One two three lift!" They heaved the metal sheet up to a standing position and Mike stepped forward, spraying insecticide in the air and on the floor.

There were four wasps sitting there, two of them already buzzing their wings, the other two sort of lurching about as they shook off the effects of having run into the metal at such a high speed. The spray misted over them and all four seemed to become more agitated, but none took off or came after any of the three men.

"Good enough!" hollered Abe, and Mike stopped spraying. Gulping in a big breath of air so that he wouldn't get any extra bug spray in his lungs, Abe jumped forward and dropped to one knee, bringing down the hammer with a solid whack on the most active-looking wasp. It took a total of three hits to kill the thing, and then he was on to the next one, and then the one after that, the whole time yelling in sequence with the whacks, "Teach-you-fuckers-to-fly-into-our-house!"

"Shit, the last bastard's gonna be a pain in the ass to catch!" yelled Ryan, while Abe still hammered at the last wasp. "Mike, come grab the metal. Quick!"

Mike jumped over Abe and grabbed hold, and then Ryan flicked the top off the fluid with his thumb and sparked the lighter with his other thumb. Already the wasp was halfway across the room, wings buzzing as it tried to take off with some little experimental hops.

He closed one eye to aim the can, and then sprayed a stream of lighter fluid at the wasp, squeezing hard to get the maximum force and distance. At the same time he slid the flame from the lighter into the stream, and felt the hot blast of air as it turned into a miniature flame thrower in the middle of his living room, like a carnival act about to go horribly wrong. A big ball of orange fire crisped the wasp, and then all three of them were in there and dancing on the floor, trying to put out the fire before it got out of hand.

A few seconds later and there were just some wisps of smoke, and then Abe was hammering on the last wasp just to make sure, while at the same time Mike and Ryan had rushed back and were trying to fit the metal into place on the window. While Mike held it up, braced on top of the other sheet, Ryan ran back to the tool bench and came out with a screwdriver and some new screws. A few minutes later and everything was back to normal, except for the chemical tang of the bug spray and the aroma of toasted wood.

"Nobody saw any others slip in?" asked Abe, sitting down on the floor, twirling the hammer in one hand.

"Nope," said Ryan. "Looks like we got off pretty easy."

"Hmmph." Mike walked over to a wall and leaned against it, slid down to the floor. "So like Abe said, maybe they're on the move already."

"So what do we do?"

"Pack up some shit and go find the web at Old Vic's," said Ryan.

"Do we bring the flame thrower and the suit?"

Ryan looked at Mike, then nodded. "Just in case, yeah, I think it's a good idea. But I'm willing to bet we end up leaving it sitting in the van." He stood back up. "Time to say goodbye to the house."

Abe stood and shrugged his shoulders. "What the hell. Not like we were going to go to far here. Bugs were trying to kill us while they were around, but I'll bet they do a better job of it by just disappearing."

They spent the next couple of hours determining what was best to take. Two backpacks and a duffle bag were soon packed to overflowing with food and survival gear and hauled to the back of the van, along with two hunting rifles and three pistols, all with plenty of extra ammunition. In the garage Ryan paused for a second, then opened his pack and grabbed two cans of bug spray from a shelf and with lots of effort and plenty of cursing managed to stuff them in. "Just in case," he said, wiping the sweat from his forehead.

Abe climbed into the front, and told Mike to come around and take the passenger seat. Ryan crawled into the back, ready to slip into the suit and heft the flame thrower if that was what was needed. And then they opened the garage door and backed up, eased out onto the road and made their way for Old Vic's place again. Immediately they could hear some soft plinks against the body of the van.

"Jesus," said Abe.

Ryan leaned up against the back of his seat. "What? What is it?"

Abe slowed down and leaned forward, peeled back a little bit of the tin that covered most of the windshield. "Would you look at that," whispered Mike.

The sky was practically covered with insects, a swarm that looked to be miles long and wide, all headed for a spot on the ground a fair distance ahead of them, like a big freaky black tornado. More bugs flew past them, not so many down near road level, but still enough to make it look like they were in the middle of a biblical plague. Butterflies flitting, beetles rumbling and bumbling, columns of ants and caterpillars marching, and more and more and more.

"How's the road?" asked Ryan.

"Not too bad. Looks like most of them are trying to keep to the sides. Guess they're smart enough to know that some bigger kids are coming to play."

"I'm getting the heebie-jeebies," said Mike. "Being around this many bugs wasn't exactly what I was thinking.

"Too late now, Mike." Ryan slapped him on his good shoulder. "We're gonna go where the little fuckers are going, good idea or not.

Besides, you've been around this many bugs all of your life; you just haven't seen them all at the same time, that's all."

Again, Abe was careful with the drive, watching out for potholes on the road, and this time also trying to steer clear of the biggest groups of bugs that didn't know any better. Too many smears on the road and he could just about guarantee that they would slide off like they were a greased bowling ball.

The sheer mass of bugs had turned the sky quite dark, but Abe could now see through the window that the sun was getting ready to set, big orange ball peaking through some gaps in the swarm. But now they were almost at Old Vic's place now, the tractor with his picked-clean skeleton parked in the field just up ahead. Smoke still rose in spots from where they had done the burn earlier, but it looked like several outbuildings were still standing, and even a few trees.

He pulled up on the side of the road just opposite the tractor, put the van in Park and let it idle. "Now what?"

Ryan leaned across the front seats and looked out through the slit. "I think we should wait. We know that most of the bugs that fly at night aren't as fast, right?"

"Right." Mike let the word draw out.

"So I think we let the sun go down, let the wasps and hornets and bees get the fuck out of the way, and then give it a bit more time for the mosquitoes to have their chance, and then we head over and go through. We'll still have some bugs to deal with, sure, but it won't be near as bad."

"You hope," said Abe. He turned the key and shut off the engine.

"I hope." Ryan sat back on the floor. "I figure we're committed now. May as well just dive in."

They sat in the van for almost four more hours, flinching every time something tinked or whapped against the side, drinking some water and munching on a couple of stale bags of chips that Abe had brought along for just this sort of reason. Outside there were sometimes other sounds, fluttering noises and clicking and rasping sounds, usually getting louder as they approached and then quieter as they passed the van by, Doppler sounds in the black of night making them feel like blind men listening to an insane chittering symphony.

"Holy shit," said Abe, looking through the slit into the night.

"What?" asked Mike.

"I can see stuff. Lights are shining and I can see a few bugs out there."

"Lights from where?" asked Ryan.

He leaned back and pulled the metal away from the side window, looked at the mirror. "A car behind us, just pulling up. And I think I see one more coming from further down the road."

"That does it then." Ryan picked up his pack and rifle and shouldered both, and then he opened the back door. He had his flashlight in hand, but left it off, as the driver of the car had left its headlights on. Abe and Mike both climbed out and came around back to get their gear.

At the same time, one man and two women climbed out of the car, and behind them a minivan pulled up, and out came a family of five, all three kids looking to be in their early to mid-teens. Four more vehicles pulled up in quick succession, more people making their way up and gathering near the headlights of the first car. "Here for the web?" asked Mike. Everyone agreed that they were.

"We'll save introductions for the other side," said Abe. "Right now seems to be a good time to go. Hell, there aren't even any bugs coming to the headlights."

"Shit," muttered the man who'd been driving the car. "Didn't even think of that." He reached in and shut off the engine, and the lights faded to black.

They all stood there letting their eyes adjust to the dark, and then Ryan said, "Follow me." And they were off.

Past the barn they could see there was some light, a glow that faded in and out. "Think that's it?" asked Abe.

"Has to be," replied Mike. "Unless someone else showed up to light some fires."

They walked until they were at the corner of the barn and then suddenly it was bright enough to see where they were going, even though they were still out of sight of the web. Mike looked up, and then pointed up into the sky. "Look at that."

They all stopped and looked up. Someone whistled softly. "What are they?" asked one of the children from the minivan.

"Fireflies," said Abe. There were huge swarms, hundreds of them, each swarm probably holding thousands of the bugs, all descending from above and blinking in patterns that carried their soft glow from one side of the sky to the other. Everyone stood still, heads tilted back, struck dumb by the absolute beauty of the silent glowing ballet above their heads.

After almost a minute, one of the women from the first car whispered, "I never thought I would ever be able to see anything from bugs as beautiful again. But this is incredible."

The patterns the bugs were creating were now like sheet lightning, only in this case without accompanying thunder, plus many of the bugs were at the moment only about a dozen feet above their heads. Rippling light washed over their faces, and they could all swear that they felt just a little bit of heat on their skin.

And then the fireflies broke into what looked like thousands of smaller groups, tight little bundles of light, and one by one they streaked off into the distance, away from the web, their abdominal lights so suddenly powerful that there was an ever-so-brief shift from yellow to red before they disappeared from sight. By the time there was only one group left, the others were just as suddenly returning, infinitesimally small flashes of blue as they zipped by on their way into the web.

Mike looked at the last group, and as he did the entire mass of fireflies floated down until they hung in the air in front of him. And then they started to blink in unison.

"It's gotta be Morse again!" shouted Ryan. "Dig out your book!"

Mike dropped the duffle bag and fished the book and a pencil from his pocket, started to write the dots and dashes on a blank spot in the back. After a couple of minutes, he saw that it was starting to repeat, and quickly started to flip through the book. The fireflies seemed satisfied with this, and with a distant-sounding *whoosh,* they too disappeared in a flash of red, only to reappear moments later in one brief blink of blue.

"Jesus," said the man from the car. "And I thought the wasps were fast. Looks like those little bastards are getting themselves up into sub-light speeds."

Mike closed the book with a snap. "Let's go," he said.

Abe stepped up beside him. "What? What did they say?"

"They said that after they go through, we've got about a half hour where it'll be just us, and that we are welcome to follow them."

"What, that's it?"

Mike shrugged. "Guess anyone who comes later has to fend for himself." He started walking, and the others fell in with him. They rounded a corner and there was the web, glowing a rainbow of colors racing up and down the spectrum. It was at least thirty feet across, bigger than lots of webs they'd seen, smaller than a few others. There was no sound, nothing from insects, nothing from the people. "That isn't all they said," Mike finally said as they stood and watched the web.

"What else?" asked Ryan.

He turned and grinned at them all, hefting his duffle bag over his shoulder. "Apparently we're going to like it over there." Then he turned and ran for the web, the others taking his cue and following close behind.

It's possible that this is the biggest stretch from this collection's self-imposed sorta theme of Us and the Environment (and don't tell me you hadn't noticed by now, even if there were no neon signs), but even though it's really sort of a pop-culture story, if you squint just right you can see it fitting in. I think.

WHAT GOES AROUND

Episode One: We meet our hero, learn a bit of his background, and leap wildly back and forth through time

The opening sequence of "Space Cops" virtually guaranteed a great audience from the very beginning. Special effects that were extremely sophisticated for the time, exciting music and fast-paced action, and of course the handsome face of star and producer Henry Angel made for great television appeal, a very new concept at the time. As well, the series was true to the beliefs of the 1950's; while fear of nuclear destruction hung over the heads of millions of Americans, the family, strong values and mostly a bright future were what they wanted to see on their primitive picture tubes each week.

Witness this portion of the opening. Before credits roll, Captain Maxwell (played by Angel) and his sidekick Corporal Exeter (played by former child radio actor Spike Chapman) board their space car and launch from the asteroid they use as headquarters. Flames jet out from the exhaust, the car tumbles wildly, bucking and heaving until, through sheer physical might, Captain Maxwell rights it and flies into the camera, the dissolve moving from space car to Maxwell to space car to Maxwell almost seamlessly.

Is it any wonder that such a nation, influenced so mightily by

> one show, would become the single most dominant space-faring country right into the late twenty-first century?
>
> —from *"Space Cops": A Modern History,* an AmeriNet 46 production

Captain Michael Davis of Sector Seven pulls himself along the rails, eschewing the artificial gravity available to him at the wave of a hand. There is an emergency in his sector, a civilian ship overrun by criminals and pirates, and he needs to get to his space car as quickly as possible. Red lights flash and alarms ring all around him.

"Davis, you there?"

Captain Davis taps his wrist, activates his comm. "Here, Slam." Slam Rankin is the dispatch officer for Sector Seven.

"There are three of them, rogues that spilled over from the Belt Wars. We managed to get good pictures before they downed the emergency activator. One of them is Marcus Heimdal."

"Thanks, Slam. Over." Heimdal! Davis picks up speed. Heimdal was the scourge of the force, but he'd gone missing four years before. Apparently to pull mercenary duty in the Belt. What was he doing back?

Private Eddie Stern is waiting in his seat in the space car when Davis arrives. They quickly check all the functions, then get clearance to launch. The roar is momentarily deafening, and they are punched back into their seats as they clear Sector Seven H.Q. The car bucks and rocks and rolls for a moment, but Davis pulls it back under control and they head off to intercept the civilian ship and the pirates aboard it.

Private Stern occupies himself with readying the weapons and checking his helmet. Nerves of steel, that boy.

They approach the civilian ship.

Henry sits in his living room, black and white TV screen flickering silently in the background, bottle of beer in hand, waiting for another visit. He knows that if he goes into his bedroom, it will happen right way, but he does not want that. In a perfect world, none of this would be happening, he wouldn't be afraid that he was losing his sanity, he wouldn't be losing himself in three cases of beer a day. In a perfect world he would have made it, wouldn't have been caught with that lighting tech and fallen into a daze of beer and whiskey, paid for by hocking furniture and crappy little jobs for shithead directors in films that no one will ever see, or ever want to see.

And a fucking crazy ghost from the future wouldn't be visiting him.

> As we see in this colorized footage of him signing autographs, Henry Angel was not only remarkably successful and popular, he was also very genial. He was especially fond of children, and often broke off early from public functions if he knew of a pick-up game of baseball being played in some nearby neighborhood. But, it must be admitted, there was a dark side to Henry Angel. He was twice-divorced, and records show that he once received a speeding ticket from the California Highway Patrol *(see: CHiPs;* Erik Estrada; 1970s). But this did not ever get in the way of his popularity.
>
> —*ibid.*

"Found him!" The voice is distant, kind of muffled.

"Hmm?"

"I said I found him. He's locked, Michael, settled and ready to pull!"

Michael switches on slomo/delay, tunes half of his view to see a representation of Arnold's face; a little fuzzy, motion not quite realtime, little mem going into receiving the visit, most being kept for the standard functions. "You're serious?"

Arnold's face jumps about as he nods; his scalp slides off and floats momentarily through the air before settling in again on his chin, a new beard. "I found him at the address we got from those old files."

"Does he know?"

A herky-jerky smile, teeth dancing a chorus line, all dressed up in perfect little tuxes. "I've been there three times now, tried to talk to him. He doesn't want to hear it, so I figure I should do the pull, explain from this side. *Fait accompli,* as it were."

"Good idea," says Mike. "I'll be out as soon as I finish running this mission."

When the ghost comes the last time for him, Henry is ready. Good and pissed, but ready. He stands, a little shakily, brushes pretzel crumbs from his shirt and pants, then stumbles forward into the receptor, glaring white light and screaming winds pounding his senses, scaring him so bad he shits his pants as he steps in and falls through time. *I mean, why the fuck not?*

Episode Two: Our hero begins to see the future as it might really be

(POV Shift: Pull camera back, encompassing view of large office area. Tangled mass of wires lead from deposit site to fuser and two well-used pocket supercomputers sitting on otherwise empty desk, walls a nondescript and unadorned brown, doors occupying three of them)

Henry staggered as he hit the floor, shuffled drunkenly for a second or two, then fell flat on his face. A pair of hands gently grabbed him around the waist and lifted him up, helped him shuffle along the floor and through a door, where he was sat upon a cot. He blinked fiercely the whole time, trying to shake the vicious light from his head, the spinning of the decades and more from his eyes.

"There's a toilet behind you," said a voice, presumably belonging to the hands. "I'll leave you for a few minutes, let you clean up. You can drop your clothes in the basket by the sink; there's a fresh uniform for you, hanging on the wall behind me." A door shut.

Henry sat for another moment to let his eyes clear, uncomfortable with the lump of stool in his pants, unable to convince himself to get up. As things slipped back into focus, he took notice of what surrounded him in the room. It was small, maybe ten feet by twelve, the walls a quiet shade of brown and the door an off-white. The cot was small, low to the ground, and didn't seem to have springs or any other metal; he felt with his hands and bent over to look, but couldn't tell what it was made of. The toilet and sink were in plain view, no door or walls to block it off. Like a prison.

The clothing hanging on the wall looked familiar. Henry stood up, with some trouble, and shuffled over to have a look.

Aw, fuck!

It was the uniform, that fucking uniform from that fucking show, the one that busted him, that caused so much shit and grief in his life. One episode and marked for life, even though couldn't be more than a few dozen people even saw the thing. Stupid show, stupid tech, stupid booze, stupid everything!

He went to the toilet, puked up the last dregs of his liquid supper, pissed, then cleaned himself. He stood there, looking at the uniform, trying to keep from shaking, and desperately wanting a beer.

> Here we see the U.S.S. *Spelling* as it drifts silently through deep space, well beyond the orbit of Jupiter. Note the sleekness of her design, the fins and grids, pods and wires, that dance from her hull like leaping, shining metallic rainbows. The gun and missile placements bristle angrily, ready to take on any and all comers, looking for an excuse to put down further armed rebellion.
>
> "This newest ship in the fleet, the pride of our armed might in space, is the replacement for the late, great U.S.S. *Tesh,* sadly lost with all hands in the gravity well of Saturn after a cowardly attack by . . .
>
> "Jesus, I'm getting all, all emotional. I'm sorry, I'm sorry, I'll be all right, but . . . those boys, they died for our country."
>
> From AmeriNet 46 *News at 0336*

After much hesitation, Henry decided to put the uniform on. It fit well, better than that piece of crap that the costume designers had come up with for the pilot. It also had the added advantage that it didn't stink like shit.

Shortly after dressing, the door cracked open tentatively, then opened wide. A man stood there, the oddest-looking man Henry had ever seen.

He was wearing a dull grey sweater that every few seconds rippled with what looked like tiny waves of oil-slick water, running in a different direction each time. His slacks were dark blue, almost black, and appeared to stiffen as the man stood still and then crack in a wild pattern of shiny crow's feet whenever he shifted a leg; he wore pale green sandals and matching socks.

He wasn't tall, this man. Maybe five foot six at best. His skin was darker than Henry's, but not so dark that he could be called a negro. Small, glittery things, like slivers of a shattered mirror, protruded from his tall forehead. He wore dark glasses that obliterated any view of his eyes, quite possibly from any angle. And his hair . . .

His hair was a wild conglomeration of wires, tubes, strings of tiny blinking lights, plastic and metal and maybe even some real hair hidden in there someplace, dark and stringy and matted in bunches under the foreign material. It was, thought Henry, as if this man had embedded his head in a Christmas tree just after a horrible soldering accident.

Upon seeing that Henry was wearing the uniform, the man broke into a huge, unrestrained grin. "Oh, this is so good to see!" said the man, accent unidentifiable but language definitely English, and he danced a few strange steps right there, Christmas lights bobbing in a sympathetic rhythm. Then he stopped and saluted Henry, a salute modeled after the style created for that stupid show; right fist to left shoulder, then open palm out, fingers facing left, elbow crooked to keep the arm half extended (didn't want to look too much like a Nazi thing).

Henry nodded in return, cautious and a little scared, especially now that the booze seemed to have unfortunately deserted his system. "Are you . . . " His voice was scratchy, so he paused to swallow, to breathe and clear some of that shit from his skull. "Are you the guy who was visiting me? From the future?"

"No!" shouted the man, sounding excruciatingly delighted and excited at this riddle. "I'm the man who visited you from the present!" At this he giggled and danced a little more; the blinking lights on his head seemed to take up a more frantic pattern, pants cracking and resetting with each step.

Episode Three: More thrilling scenes
from this week's episode

Captain Michael Davis, fresh from his heroic encounter with Marcus Heimdal (currently on his way to serving a thirty-year sentence at the Charon Penal Colony—let's see him bust out of there!) has raced back to

Earth with the aid of the newest in space travel technology. Less than a day to get there, as opposed to the two months it used to take, laughing in the face of modern physics.

A quick slingshot around the Moon, using its gravity to slow down rather than speed up (trust us on this), then captured by the Earth's gravity, sinking into a low orbit that makes parking on a dime after slowing down from 300 miles per hour in only four feet look easy. Private Stern gives him the thumbs-up. Perfect positioning.

A quick check of instruments, and then communicate with headquarters back in good old U.S. of A. Salt Lake City, to be exact, taking over where Hollywood left off after it sank beneath the waves.

"Captain Michael Davis, Sector Seven, to Sector One Headquarters, requesting permission to land."

A brief pause, and then, "Permission granted, Captain Davis. And congratulations on a job well done."

The strange man interrupted his equally strange dance to mumble something unintelligible, the Christmas lights blinking ever more fiercely. Then he grinned at Henry. "Come with me, please."

Henry followed him out of the room, shuffling along nervously. They walked through another room (previously described) and the strange man (whose name was Arnold, although there is no way that Henry could yet know that), bypassed the desk and the mass of wires and opened the door on the far side of that room.

Still following, Henry saw that another man was there, similarly attired and wearing dark and very large goggles, sitting in something like a dentist's chair, more wires and gimcracks protruding from his head, as well as several tubes leading from his arms and one even coming from his belly. The wires led to a receptacle in the wall, the tubes to a metal and plastic and something-else contraption sitting hunched beside the chair, humming along to itself in ever-changing pitches.

Private Stern disappears, replaced by Arnold, all fuzzy and grainy and jerky again, a cheap representation of his real self. Bits of skin slag off and drift for a moment before reattaching themselves; one eye-ball drifts away for a moment, before Arnold can capture it with his tongue, all four feet of it.

"Darn it, I wish you wouldn't do that!"

"He's here, Michael," says Arnold, ignoring the admonition. "Time to come on down."

Arnold reached over and touched a button on the humming machine. "He's here, Michael. Time to come on down." The machine shuddered and spit and whistled and belched and even barfed some sort of grayish fluid onto the floor, which was promptly cleaned up by four small cartoonish brooms with arms, each carrying two very real wooden buckets. Henry blinked his eyes, unsure where they had come from, and when he looked again they were gone, as was the barf.

The tubes withdrew, some going from arms to machine and some from machine into the arms, the (slightly larger) one in the belly pulling out from there and being sucked into the machine, accompanied by the sort of slurping noise one associates with a child eating spaghetti. The wires disentangled themselves, and pulled into a slot in the wall or else wrapped themselves around Michael's skull, a cheerful rainbow of Medusan snakes settling in for a nap.

The space car lands, magnificent Salt Lake City's towers thrusting into the sky all around it, like fingers reaching for God. Captain Michael Davis reaches out, touches a button, and watches the car and the city dissolve around him, fading to nothing. He turns his head, gazes with fondness and consternation at Arnold, with definite capital-A Awe at Henry. Time to sit up.

Episode Four: A brief hysterical interlude

(POV Shift: Swing camera in close, closer, closest. Burrow deep into the skull, sneak the camera past the blood-brain barrier, find your way along the neurons, synapses firing and sparking at a savage rate, pretend you have a wondrous device to translate what follows)

—Oh God oh Christ I can't believe what the fuck is happening to me here. Maybe maybe maybe this is only a dream, maybe I got the fucking deetees, maybe I'm gonna wake up in a few minutes and laugh at all this. Noise in my head buzzing that's gotta be it—

—Shit no I'm still here these guys are for real maybe they aren't even from the future maybe they're aliens or something, come to grab me from their flying saucer—

—Calm down, don't let them see you scared. Maybe they can smell fear like dogs or something—

—Shit—

Episode Five: Your trip to the outer reaches made easy

Michael stood up, pants cracking to allow him access to the floor, stiffening to keep him up. He hawked and spit on the floor, phlegm and a little bit of blood mixing, but not enough to worry about, cleared his throat a couple of times.

"Tired?" ventured Arnold.

Michael nodded. "Long trip," he rasped. "Good one, though." They hugged.

"Mmm," said Arnold, pulling away after a second. "Michael, I would like you to meet Henry Angel, himself. Mr. Angel, this is Michael Davis, your number one fan, I am sure."

Henry reached out a hand to shake, stared at empty air for a moment as Michael did not proffer his own. Then he dropped his arm and nodded. "Please. Call me Henry." *What the hell is going on here?*

"I am delighted to meet you, Henry," said Michael. "Your life as Captain Maxwell has been an inspiration to me and to tens of millions of other Americans."

Henry couldn't take it any longer. "What are you talking about? I played in that stupid show for one fucking episode! No one saw it except for some jerks at the network who decided that it would cost too much and I was too big a risk!"

Both men smiled. Arnold nodded sagely and said, "Experience is every bit as fluid as time, Henry." This seemed to greatly amuse both of them. Arnold danced that little dance, and Michael jigged for a brief moment as well, though it seemed to tire him out quite quickly.

Episode Six: Henry's life as it otherwise might have been

With the help of two of his few remaining good friends, Henry was taken to a doctor who saw fit to enroll him in a health spa that specialized in people with Henry's problem. Three months of intense physical and emotional work paid off, and Henry left the spa drier than he'd ever been since coming to Hollywood.

Rumors stuck like glue, however, and Hollywood would have nothing to do with him, so he left town and moved back home, lived in the basement of his mother's house on a farm in Sonoma County. By day he did carpentry, working for an old friend of his father's who built houses. By night, he put together a small community theater, put on some performances that were okay, some that were pretty awful, and a few that were terrific.

In the early seventies some of his roles in some especially atrocious B-grade horror films were rediscovered, and he was invited back to Hollywood to do some work in a few small productions, even some guest spots on some series television. He wanted more, however, and couldn't attain it.

Resentment of his situation and fear about his true self served to put him back on the downward spiral. Booze showed up again, this time accompanied by cocaine and other drugs.

Henry died of heart failure in 1976, two days after he had begun filming a guest spot in a popular detective series. Seven people attended his funeral.

Henry dried up, got some great parts, ended up copping an Oscar for a supporting role, went on to a life of acclaim as a character actor. A few months after coming out of the closet, he died at age sixty-eight, drowned in a boating accident.

Henry stayed in Sonoma County, got the house when his mother died, married his childhood sweetheart, raised a good family, then, still lost in his past and confused about who he really was, blew his brains out in 1972.

Henry stayed in Sonoma County, got the house, married his childhood sweetheart, raised a good family, then got a divorce. He died at age eighty-five, his two surviving children at his bedside. The construction company he had built with his father's old friend was worth tens of millions.

Episode Seven: Why Part Six doesn't really matter

The explanation is almost more than Henry can bear. He has been flung through time and greeted by people who, while undeniably human, have more than a few weird things counting as strikes against them.

And now he has heard a tale unlike anything he ever expected to hear: Now, in this future, Henry Angel is a hero. Honest to God, bigger than life. Michael and Arnold show him little snippets of television, or at least something very similar to it, shows that concentrate on him, but on a life he never led.

But how could he have led this life? Henry asks this, but the answers are not remotely satisfactory.

It is a fluid life, Arnold says, or a neurologically experiential one. It has been created, says Michael, with the aid of the net. Michael doesn't elaborate.

Besides, says Arnold, time is what you make of it. And we are running out of time to make, so we need you here. He pauses, grins, dances a little bit more, and then asks if Henry would like to experience the net.

Um, delays Henry, does experiencing this net have anything to do with those things in my body and on my head?

Another dance, and then heads nod gleefully, lights and wires bobbing.

Henry turns and runs, not knowing where the hell he's going, but knowing it has to be away from here.

Episode Eight: Henry's visit to the big city and a partial inventory of the things he sees

Buildings. Buildings, buildings, buildings and buildings. Some abandoned machines, look sort of like cars or something. More buildings.

Some streetlights. None of them working, though.

Pavement, cracked and weathered. Weeds growing out of the cracks. No people, no birds, no insects.

The sky, what Henry can see with all the tall buildings (did we mention all the buildings?) in the way, is gray, disturbed, distant and cold.

No sound, aside from a far-off hum, alien and probably unattainable.

Once, maybe, a person, far away down a street, half hidden in shadows. Said person doesn't respond to shouts, and, exhausted after running and yelling the entire distance, Henry's arrival at the approximate location reveals nothing.

Except for more buildings.

Episode Nine: The real world

Henry sat on the cold pavement, leaning against one of the gray buildings that marched down the streets like so many monoliths. Shaking from exhaustion and fear, he leaned his head back and watched the sky for a few moments, wondering at the total absence of blue sky, of clouds.

He may have fallen asleep. The new sound seemed to intrude on his dreams first, unsettled visions of dancing Christmas trees and much-needed bottles of beer. A growl superseded that, distant and dreamlike at first, then persistent enough to get his attention.

"Henry."

He blinked his eyes open, stood up with a start. In front of him, on the street, was a vehicle of some sort.

"Henry," came the voice again. It was Arnold, inside the vehicle.

"What?"

"Oh, thank goodness, it *is* you. It took me forever to find this cab, and it isn't hooked up as well as it might have been a few decades ago. Please climb in." A side door slid open.

"Why? Why should I go back?"

"You can't go back, Henry. That's the problem. We pulled you up, but it was a one way trip. You are stuck now, and you're going to have to live with it."

Henry shook his head. "Then why'd you bring me here? This is hell!"

Arnold chuckled, a gentle sound this time. "You were in hell before, Henry. You weren't going to live for much longer. Please climb in and I'll explain."

Perhaps relieved to get away from the oppressive bulk of the buildings and from the all-encompassing grayness that surrounded him, Henry complied. He sat down, the door sliding shut behind him. But there was no one else in the vehicle.

"Where are you?" he asked as it started to move.

"Back where I've always been," said Arnold. "That's why it took so long to find you. I couldn't track down a cab that was operable. Most of them have just been sitting and rusting for years, decades, centuries even."

Henry nodded, not exactly sure of what Arnold was saying but not wanting anymore details. "You said you'd explain."

"I did indeed," said Arnold, his voice coming from in front as well as to the sides. The vehicle grumbled and complained for a second, and then lurched forward. Peaceful piano music played from somewhere behind Henry's head.

"We live in tough times, Henry. Very difficult for all of us. The world that you knew came to an end a very long time ago, and our struggles to make do have pretty much been for nothing." The vehicle turned a corner a little too hard. "Sorry about that," said Arnold. "These mesh controls are old and rusty, and covered with dust and dead bugs. I'm just surprised they were never cannibalized."

"You were saying . . ." prompted Henry.

"Oh yes. Your future, my past, we fucked up. I won't go into a litany of things that went wrong. If you want you can do your own investigating when the time comes. Let's just say that this isn't a very pretty world.

"People being people, they want to hide from things when they aren't very pretty. Hiding in your time meant beer, whiskey, that sort of thing. Right?"

Henry nodded. He'd been good at hiding near the end, there.

"Well, these days people have stories, events, whole lives they lead outside of reality. This thing we call the net—and no, I have no idea why we call it that—takes people into these lives, lets them experience them just like they were real."

Another corner. The background piano music swelled briefly, then faded back again. Arnold continued.

"Someone, many years ago, got their hands on the pilot you made, the 'Space Cops' thing. Turned it into a whole event, this grand series that changed the way America and the world was." He sighed. "A lovely story, really. There was even a fabulous version of you wandering around the net, interacting with all sorts of people whenever they wanted, although most people were happy being the heroes themselves.

"Not all of us were caught up in the scenario, however, although I must admit even for people like me it is difficult to spend more than a few hours away from it. I myself worked with some others on a device to bring someone through time, a kind of a hobby thing based on some old math one of us found drifting in a file somewhere, which explains how you got here. Not that any of us actually expected it to work."

"Where are the other people you worked with?" asked Henry.

Arnold chuckled. "I don't know. To tell you the truth, the chances are very good that they don't exist, or perhaps they did, but now they don't."

"Huh?"

"Never mind," said Arnold. "I'm just finding it harder and harder to figure out who's who these days. Maybe because I'm thinking about it now. I don't know."

"Why'd you bring me here?" Henry was feeling very confused.

"To put it bluntly, Henry, I'm losing Michael. He's spending more and more time away from me, and I don't have the energy in me to traipse all the way around a virtual solar system trying to keep up with him. I was kind of hoping your presence would be a nifty gift for him."

"A gift? You brought me forward in time to be a present?" Henry shook his head, feeling a dull ache beginning to creep up from his shoulders to his skull. Nothing in his life had been as confusing as the way Arnold behaved and spoke.

"Well, that and something for all of our society to look to. We need inspiration, Henry, inspiration to make more of ourselves. You can be that inspiration!"

The vehicle stopped and the door slid open. They were in a large empty warehouse, parked under a feeble pool of light cast by the only two fitfully-working bulbs that were hanging from the high ceiling. Arnold walked into the light to greet Henry as he got up from his seat and stepped out.

"How can a broken-down drunk be inspiration?" asked Henry.

"You can be so because we made you so!" said Arnold. "Come join us." He almost whispered this last.

Henry shook his head. "No. I want to go home."

Arnold grimaced. "You can't, even if I could let you. I'm sorry that's your answer."

There was a distant whine near Henry's ear, a mosquito maybe, although he'd not seen or heard any insects up until now, and then he felt a small sting in his neck. He swatted at it, but already things were going dim. As he fell forward, he managed to focus for a brief second on the gurney that rushed up to break his fall.

Episode Ten: The Henry Effect

The space car comes in for as smooth a landing as can be expected, considering the circumstances. "You're in," comes the distant voice of

Slam Rankin, now promoted to Sector One. "Good luck."

"Thanks."

He steps out, views the unfamiliar landscape, almost alien in proportions. Buildings are too small and spaced too far apart, the riot of colors is almost too much for his unaccustomed eyes.

And there are more lights here than last time—a bad sign. Too many more joining this and the Space Cops will collapse. There is also no movement at all, and the silence is a different sort of quiet, unlike anything he has ever experienced in his life.

The walk is a short one, due to the space car being able to land in such small areas. Trees, scorched by the passing rockets, are already healing themselves, fast motion, almost liquid as they turn from shriveled and black to gray to erect and brown and green.

The entrance is open to him. After a pause to collect his thoughts, he steps across the threshold and into the room. They are there, the two of them, sitting as he expected to find them.

Henry looks up. "Arnold! So good to see you! Come in, come in."

Michael looks up from the nonsense patterns playing on the screen, smiles when he sees Arnold. He waves the hand that is not holding the bottle of beer, grinning. "Hiya Arnold. Been watching you on TV." With the hand holding the beer he gestures at the black and white screen.

Henry gets up and walks to another room, comes out holding a second bottle of beer, which he hands to Arnold. Arnold's protests that he is on duty are ignored.

When they are all settled in on the couch and chairs Henry smiles and says, "Good life you brought me to, Arnold. And I sure like what you've done to my old show."

Arnold is about to say something, but the nonsense on the screen fades and he is hushed. "The show's back on," says Michael. "Wait until the next commercial."

Arnold shrugs his shoulders, takes a sip of the beer, and leans back to watch himself, Henry and Michael sitting in a room drinking beer and watching TV.

All up and down the street, thousands of others share in the experience. Ratings go through the roof.

Eventually, Arnold goes and grabs another beer, settles down to enjoy the show.

Maybe some day a student of Alberta politics will read this story and figure out what the hell is going on. In the meantime, the Train is inspired (but not ripped off, never that) by Richard Grant's marvelous novel Through the Heart, *and I wish he was writing lots more cool stuff.*

BLUE TRAIN

An explosion shattered the silence, and after a moment Andy saw a plume of smoke and dust rise up from behind a distant hill. "Anyone else supposed to be out prospecting in this area?"

"Negative," said his quad. "I'm attempting to patch into a network satellite, see if I can get a fix on what's over there."

Andy collapsed his sleeping bag and stuffed it into a saddlebag, took a last swig of strong Indian tea, then hopped onto the quad, battered cup still in hand. "To hell with the network. So many birds going down, that could take hours before you get an idea what's happening.

"What's over there is using explosives. If you insist on going to look, then I would ask that you please leave me behind. My sense of self-preservation has certainly not been depleted by your rough treatment."

"Shut up," said Andy, flipping open the control panel and tapping at a gauge. "Your battery is still at forty-five percent, so we'll run electric and leave the fuel for later. Quieter that way." He thumbed a button and turned the throttle, and the quad jumped forward with a rising hum.

"That hill will likely leave my battery at less than twenty percent, Andy."

"And the sun is already out. Start recharging and stop worrying."

They drove across the dry creek bed, the quad steering them to the part of the opposite bank that looked easiest to mount. From there it was a steady ride up the hill, tacking back and forth to avoid tipping over, Andy leaning hard uphill each time to help with balance. As they neared the crest, there was another explosion, much louder this time.

Andy let the throttle snap back to off, and the quad slid to a stop on a small plateau near the top, parked beneath a sickly stand of aspen. He reached back and grabbed his old binoculars, then jumped off and hurried up the hill.

He dropped to his belly at the top and, using a bush as cover, snuck a look. "Fuck," he whispered. "Last thing I wanted to see out here."

Less than fifty meters away just past the bottom of the hill sat a sniffer, settled down in a low crouch on all six legs. In front of its battered metal and ceramic body was a large gash in the earth. A look with the binoculars confirmed what the sniffer was looking for; moisture was beginning to pool, flowing from the water table that Andy had been scouting.

He crawled backwards down the hill until he was sure he would be out of sight of the device, and then stood and skidded the rest of the way down to the quad. "Find a network yet?" he asked.

"Nothing," replied his machine. "What's over there?"

"A sniffer. It found the water."

There was a pause. Then, "That isn't good. Without a network we can't register this find. Anything on the side or top of the sniffer to tell you to whom it belongs?"

"I didn't stay around long enough to really look. Figured I'd come down first and see if there was a way we could beat it to the punch."

"Go back up and look, first, see if you can make out any markings on the side. Come back down and tell me what you see, and I'll cross-reference that and then we'll know what sort of chance we stand to save this claim."

Andy nodded, turned and ran back up the hill. The sniffer was still sitting in place, which might have been a good sign, but might not have been one as well. It could have been using this time to recharge some batteries, or it could have been in contact with its own network. If the second was true, then it had access to much better resources than Andy, and besides already registering this claim would be able to cause Andy no end of trouble if he tried anything.

Some of the ID on the side of the sniffer was illegible, scorched by previous blasts or worn away by time and weather. He was able to make out a string of six letters and numbers, though, as well as what looked like a faded picture of a star riding above what looked like a bear, only with something wrong with it.

He was about to sneak back down out of sight when a glint of sunlight in the distance caught his eye.

Leaning back down on his elbows, he maxed out the mag on his binoculars and focused in on a giant gleaming silver snake, riding on large wheels and coming slowly his way.

"Oh, shit."

Back down the hill, then, faster than the last time. He almost fell as he tried to stop by the quad, but he managed to grab the bag rack on the back, almost ripping his arm out of its socket in the process.

"What is it?" asked the machine. "Why the rush?"

Andy climbed on and throttled the quad up, driving downhill as fast as he dared. He was too busy concentrating on not tumbling over that he didn't answer.

"My battery is only at twenty-five percent, Andy," warned the quad. "If you don't switch over to fuel soon, we won't be going anywhere and I won't even be around to talk to you."

"Whiner," said Andy. The quad was silent, likely pouting in response.

They finally came to a stop after climbing and descending one more hill. Andy got off the quad and paced for a moment before finally sitting on the ground in front of the machine.

"There's a pipeline coming. Maybe two klicks away at the outside."

"Already? There's something wrong with that sort of speed. What were you able to read on the side of the sniffer?"

"A bunch of the numbers or letters were pretty much erased. I was able to get 7Q6-CA-6, as well as a picture of a star sitting above a bear that looked like it had a tumor on its back."

"Ah," said the quad. "That certainly explains a lot, as well as opening up some new questions."

Looking up at where the sun had managed to crawl in the past ten minutes, Andy opened his pouch and pulled out a small pot of sunscreen and started smearing it on his face. "Tell me just what it explains," he said, wiping an extra-thick layer across his nose.

"American," answered the machine. "Judging by your description of the seal, I'd say the animal was probably a grizzly bear, so this would have come up from California."

Andy stopped, cocked an eyebrow back at the quad. "Grizzly bear? What the hell's that?" But before he could get an answer, another thought occurred to him. "And there's no fucking way that can be an American sniffer and pipeline! Shit, nobody even pays attention to where the border is anymore, but we sure as hell aren't so close that the two of those would crawl all this way for water! Especially from, from . . ." He snapped his fingers, trying to remember.

"California. And you're right, Andy, they wouldn't crawl all this way. Likely a pumping station has been set up, in Montana or in Idaho Free State to get it over the Rockies, or even on our side of the border."

"Well shit," whispered Andy. "Couldn't be our side. Enough gunfire over water rights on either side of the border without bringing it an international flavor."

"Most states are now cooperating, Andy," replied the quad. "It is equally difficult for all of them these days."

"Hmph. No network yet?"

"Nothing. I begin to wonder if any incoming signals are being deliberately blocked or scrambled."

Andy sat back down on the quad. "Why would that be?"

"It is a good chance they aren't allowed to be here. Unlikely that they have signed any sort of agreement with the feds, but that's the only way they should be allowed to get an extraction deal."

Andy laughed. "I don't see the feds sticking their noses in anything out here anymore."

"A signal, Andy! Wait one moment," said the quad. Andy stood silent, nervously rubbing his fingers on his palms while he waited.

"That wasn't the network. The pipeline is almost in place, and was broadcasting its claim. Says it has permission of the Blue Train to be here."

"Son of a bitch!" Andy kicked at a rock, sent it caroming off one of the quad's tires and into some squat bushes nearby. "Who the fuck do those provincial assholes think they are, giving permission for something like this? They pull up stakes and head out for no one knows the fuck where, and next thing you know they're cutting deals they aren't allowed to cut to give away our water. My water."

"The message repeated twice and then went dead. Still no access. I'm now fairly sure that I'm being blocked from getting at it."

"Fine." Andy started rummaging through the field equipment box that sat strapped to the back of the quad.

"What are you looking for?"

"Gonna take care of this myself," he answered. "I don't give a shit if it's the Blue Train or not, and I sure as hell don't care about the Americans." Andy pulled out three chunks of explosive and detonators, slipped them into two different vest pockets, then pulled his old rifle out of its holster and shouldered it.

"You can't be serious," said the quad. "You have no idea what will come down on your head if you get caught. When you get caught. At the very least, you lose any chance you have to claim this water."

"Doesn't matter. I want you to be ready to broadcast this location to the network as soon as that block is dropped. Tell everyone there's a new lake been found." He dug out an extra box of bullets, tucked it into a pants pocket.

"A lake? Andy, I don't know what you are talking about, but any call like that will bring in prospectors from miles and miles around. Probably bring in ordinary folk, too, if they're stupid enough to still be living out on the land." The machine paused for a second. "And it occurs to me that if the Blues signed a deal to give up water rights, they might be bold enough to sign a deal to try and circumvent fed jurisdiction with extradition."

"There you go with the feds again. Look, the Blues don't run this province anymore; they gave up that right when they packed up and headed out on that goddamn Train of theirs."

"But they are still the nominal power in these parts, since no one sees any sign of the feds at all these days. And back to the topic at hand, all American and former American states have the death penalty for anyone who sabotages their water supplies. The feds historically wouldn't ship anyone south if they face hanging or the firing squad, but based on philosophy the Blue Train may not feel so concerned for their own nominal citizens."

Andy shrugged. "Still my fucking water. If I'm going to give it up, everyone gets it. Took years of looking through charts and maps and infrareds we cheated from those birds in orbit to find a spot where the table had come back up. And I'm not gonna lose it to some mechanical pirates from another country."

The machine made a sound like a sigh. "Very well. You can't do this alone, then." A small dark green metal box spit out of the side of the quad and landed on the ground. "That's my beacon. I've tied it to a . . ." The machine paused, made a sound eerily like a shudder. "To a deadman's switch I've just programmed. I can set it off if need be, but if I become incapacitated while following you around like a fool, it will start to broadcast a signal. It gives the approximate coordinates for this magical new lake of yours."

"You don't have to do this, you know," Andy told the quad. "I'm sure I can figure out some way of getting to them."

"Unlikely. The sniffer won't be expecting anyone, but it also won't just let you walk up and attach some plastic explosives to it, and those bullets won't do anything but ricochet off its body and maybe bounce back to put a big ugly hole in you."

"So what do you propose?"

"Leave your gun. How steep do you think that hill is leading down to the sniffer?"

"Fairly steep. No way you can ride straight down there. You'd tip and roll, likely squash me flat."

"Exactly what I thought," said the quad. "But what if I went around the side of the hill with my engine roaring? Do you think you could do a decent tuck and roll?"

Andy scratched his beard, picturing the process. "Not too many trees in the way, or big rocks. It'll hurt, but I think I could do it without too much pain. But I'm gonna be dizzy as hell when I get to the bottom."

"Good point. I keep forgetting that the limits on humans just don't seem to end."

"But I see where you're going with this," said Andy, "and I think I see a way around it. Just trust me on it, and do your level best to divert the sniffer's attention. Give me thirty seconds after I wave at you from the top, all right? I don't know how well I can time this."

"Climb aboard then," replied the quad. "I'll take you to the bottom of the hill. But don't you start until you know I'm in place."

The quad brought him back to the hill, then headed off to the east, leaving Andy to lean hard and run up the slope as best as he could. Just short of the top he pulled out one chunk of explosive and inserted a detonator into it, held on to it tight. Then he double-checked his pocket to make sure that the remote for the detonator was still there.

Finally, he peeked over the edge and down the hill. The sniffer was still sitting in place, and the pipeline was now set up by the hole the sniffer had made. It was drilling deeper, braces having dropped down to keep its front wheels from moving anywhere. Already he could hear the motors as the powerful miniature pumps inside the pipeline started pulling the water up from underground.

He stood and waved to the quad, took a deep breath, then dove headfirst over the top of the hill, hanging tight to the explosives and the detonator. The first roll on the rocky soil knocked the breath right back out of him, a big whoosh of air that he could feel but not hear; the only sounds he could make out were the rustling of his clothes and the thumps and bumps and cracks as his body and head hit dirt and rocks and dried branches. He tried to keep his eyes closed, but they kept opening on their own, giving him a stomach-churning view of harsh blue sky swiftly followed by baked brown earth, and then repeated again and again.

And then he hit a small bump and went spinning into the air, rolled to a stop face up on the ground, hot sun trying to burn its way through his eyelids. He stayed still, feeling every muscle in his body trying to twitch, feeling the agony of the bruises, but thankfully not finding anything that felt like a broken bone.

Andy could hear the sniffer walking towards him now as he played dead, steady thumps reverberating through the ground and into his skull with background accompaniment from the pipeline as it pulled his precious water from the below. He had kept a tight grip on the explosive and the detonator, kept his fists closed as the American machine approached.

There was a loud roar off in the distance and then a shuffling as the sniffer shifted itself to view the quad. Andy opened his eyes and saw that it was turned the other way now, about three meters from him, and he rolled quickly to his knees and then jumped up, with two quick steps getting to the sniffer and slapping the explosive charge onto its body and then turning and running as fast as his dizzy state would allow.

One quick look behind showed that it had turned and was following him; too close to set off the charge, really, but if he waited any longer it would be closer still, or would catch him and then put in a call for help. He thumbed the trigger button.

There was a loud bang and then a sort of double-*whumpf,* and Andy was thrown to the ground. Something slammed into his back, once again knocking the wind out of him, and immediately after he felt something slice through his forearm. The heat on his back was fierce, even worse than the sun at noon.

Rolling onto his back, Andy held up his arm and had a look at the damage; nothing too serious, more of a scratch than anything, he decided. A small cloud of smoke hung in the still air and some of the scrub was on fire now, but the flames were small and already burning themselves down.

He sat up, put his hands to his ears to try and block out the ringing that started there, and watched as the quad rolled up to him. There were some muffled sounds coming from it, but nothing he could make out.

"Shit, I guess that thing still had some explosives inside it," he said. His voice sounded muffled, like he was talking with his mouth full of cloth.

More sounds from the quad. He waved his arms and shook his head, winced and put a hand to his forehead. "Can't hear a damn thing, quad. The explosion must've done something to my ears." He looked over to the pipeline, which appeared to be undamaged. "You getting through to the network now? Roll backwards a bit if yes." The machine rolled backwards. "Sending out the message I wanted you to?"

It stayed still.

Andy reached forward and grabbed a handlebar, pulled himself up and leaned heavily on the quad. "Well why the fuck not?" He yawned, felt a popping in his ears. "Sounds like . . ." He grinned. "Good. Hearing's coming back. Now, why the fuck not?"

"Climb on me and I'll show you," said the quad, still sounding distant.

"In a minute." Andy reached into his pocket, pulled out the other two chunks of explosive and detonators, and started running for the pipeline. He heard the quad rev up and start following him.

There was a good point about fifteen meters away from the snout and drill of the pipeline, sitting just back of another set of giant wheels. He got there and bent over, trying to catch his breath and feeling all of the new pains from the past few minutes. When he looked back up the quad was back beside him.

"I'm sending out the message now, but I'm not happy about it," it said. "You need to hurry and do this, though. I've got something to show you and then we have to get out of here."

"Right." Andy reached up, but the pipeline was still well beyond his hand. He tried jumping, but couldn't get much height with all of his muscle aches. He turned to the quad. "Come here, closer."

The machine moved to a place under the pipeline, and Andy climbed up and stood on the seat. Reaching high and standing on his toes, he was able to stick the charge to the battered gray metal pipe. He squatted down and grabbed the handlebar, told the quad to move another meter down the line, then he stood up and attached the other explosive, just in case. In the distance, the pipeline marched on through a gap in the low hills that surrounded them. A perfect place for a lake.

"Okay," he said, sitting down and grabbing a handle with one hand, pulling the detonator out of his pocket with the other. "Show me what you think I need to see, and let's get this done with."

The quad gunned its engine and they tore back up the hill Andy had just rolled down. Halfway up he yelled "Stop!" and then turned and pressed the button. Two simultaneous blasts pierced the air, chunks of metal flying high into the sky, and then a great gout of water began to spew forth from the pipeline, spilling out onto the parched earth. More water than Andy had ever seen, and all of it pouring free.

He tapped the side of the quad's fuel tank. "Show me."

The engine roared to life again, and soon they were at the top of the hill. Andy sat for a second, mouth hanging open, watching what approached from the west, and then dismounted and stood beside the quad.

"Haven't seen that in twenty years, maybe more." His voice was almost a whisper. "How long do you figure we have?"

"Less than an hour, I would guess. Can't outrun it, though. It got a fix on us as soon as I found my way back onto the network."

In the distance, towering above the tallest trees this parched land had to offer, the Blue Train was coming. Too distant to hear, its visage wavered in the hot air, a mirage one moment, more solid the next.

Andy shrugged, suddenly aware that the fight had finally left him. "We'll stay here, then. Wouldn't want to leave my lake without seeing how it turns out, anyway."

He sat painfully on the ground and leaned against a tire. Sometimes Andy would turn his head and watch as the Blue Train continued its approach, growing ever-larger and more foreboding by the minute, but more often he sat and watched the water pour forth, already a good-sized pond, arcing out and then splashing down from the wrecked pipeline like some mythical fountain, sunlight reflecting brilliantly off the water, mesmerizing in its unfamiliarity. Soil was stirring up underneath, giving most of the pond a dark and muddy look, but now Andy could see that in the center, at its deepest, it was starting to reflect the pure stark blue of the sky.

Eventually a deep rumble began to overtake the sound of the dancing waters, something Andy felt in his bones and teeth before he could really hear, but becoming more audible with each moment. Finally he had no choice but to turn and watch the Blue Train, remembering that when it was present there was nothing that could overwhelm it.

There were eight cars now; the last time he'd seen it there were only five, rushing past in the distance and still large enough to blot out the mountains that had sat behind it. Twenty years ago it had still carried that new sheen, sparkling and shining in the harsh light of the day, metal gleaming in a way that was both uplifting and vaguely threatening.

Today there was nothing vague about the feeling. The Train was huge, menacing, almost angry-looking. Any polish it had once carried had been lost to the elements and the years, and now, even from this distance Andy could see the rust and grease and soot that pockmarked its surface, the rusted-out holes that ran along the bottom.

"It looks nothing like the pictures I see over the network," said the quad.

Andy shook his head, trying to force away the fear he felt in the pit of his stomach. "I guess we all change, don't we? Maybe not on the inside, but sure as hell do on the outside."

The Train began to slow down now, hissing and screeching with angry blasts of steam as it broke its way through small stands of quivering aspen and dipped and rose over smaller hills. Dry earth split and cracked beneath its wheels, small boulders shattered under its weight, and as it finally came to a complete stop a blast of extra-hot air sent a wave of dry soil across Andy and the quad. It shuddered and roared for a few seconds, and then with one last string of noisy farts, the engine fell silent.

For minutes the only sounds were the gurgling of the slowly growing lake and the squeaks, moans and hisses of the Blue Train as it settled. Andy just sat on the ground, watching and waiting, wiping grit from his eyes, nervously drumming his fingers and chewing on his lip.

Although the Train had come to rest at the bottom of the hill where Andy was, its peak was almost equal to that of the hill. The engine was larger than the other cars, over eighty meters long, and its wheels, dozens of them, each stood three times his height. Every wheel had a flaw of some sort, and some were so badly worn down that they didn't even touch down to the ground, were held up by the others to spin fruitlessly in the air. Deadfall stuck out at odd angles from various holes, and there was even the rotting corpse of a deer impaled on a stray piece of rusting metal.

The car behind the engine was only a bit smaller, dozens of rows of windows reaching from bottom to top. From some windows Andy could see faces peering briefly out before hiding back in the shadows, the mysteries of their lives and tasks intact for the moment.

A loud squeal interrupted the silence, and a door opened at the bottom of the first car, metal grinding against metal. Two men, tiny figures dwarfed by the Train, jumped to the ground and then pulled out two slats of rust and white metal, laid them down to be a ramp. There was an echoing growl from inside the car, and then a real automobile exited from the darkness, descended to the ground and started up the hill.

"What is it?" asked Andy.

"A Jeep," answered the quad.

Andy stood and held his hand over his eyes to keep the sun out. A real Jeep, driving up the hill toward him. Two miracles in one day. He looked down at the quad, wondering if he should try to make a break for it now, knowing as the thought touched his mind that he wouldn't get halfway down the hill. He steeled himself and continued to watch its approach.

The driver gave the accelerator an extra touch as it crested the hill, and then spun the wheel and brought the Jeep to rest beside them. Two men carrying guns immediately jumped out, muzzles pointing at the ground but with their threat clearly implied. Then the driver also climbed out, running around to the other side and opening the door for his last passenger, standing back as that man stepped to the ground.

The first three men were all dressed in gray and brown camo, but this last man wore the uniform of the Blues, gray pants with only one or two small patches, a similar jacket, a light blue shirt and a red tie. His hair was also gray, perfectly combed, and he was freshly shaved. His teeth were white and even; his smile never wavered, seemed to be pasted on his face. For a few seconds he stood and watched the lake, then turned and looked at Andy. "It is a beautiful sight, isn't it?"

Andy blinked. He hadn't expected polite conversation, even if this man was a politician. "The lake? Yeah, it is. Never seen anything like it."

The Blue seemed to find this amusing. His smile grew even more, and he glanced back at his driver and the two men with guns, who also smiled. "Then perhaps you should find your way further north some day. There are still some small streams there, and even ponds that have not gone stagnant. And yes, a nice lake or two."

Andy shrugged. "I've heard stories. I'm also told that high in the mountains there are still some crystal-clear lakes and streams, and even some animals to be found. Not as if that does either of us any good."

"Yes. Sadly, the Train won't let us take our government into the mountains," said the Blue. "Too big. Pacifica claims that land now, you know, and holds back what water they can."

"Then why give this water up to the Americans? If you can't get any of that water that used to belong to us, then why not take advantage of the water that we do find here?"

"Oh, we wrote off this area long ago. Most of the south. Since the Exodus boarded the Train we've concentrated on our resources north of the Dry Zone."

"You've given over the south half of the province," said the quad.

The Blue's smile faltered for a fraction of a second, but a blink of his eyes seemed to reset it. "Ah, his machine speaks. I keep forgetting that before the Train departed we still allowed intelligent machines." He looked back to Andy. "Your device is correct. We have ceded territory over to our friends to the south, in exchange for some future, ah, considerations." He smiled, as if at a secret joke. "So now we will wait until our friends can muster a replacement pipeline, as well as officers to take you south for your trial and likely execution. I think we will have plenty of room on a lower level of a rear car, and I'm sure that your ATV will have parts we can use."

"You have no jurisdiction," replied the quad.

Now the man frowned. "I didn't come here to argue with a machine," he said. "The feds have no business here anymore, no longer even poke their heads west of Lake Winnipeg. And as the Deputy Minister of External Affairs, it is my job to make sure things run smoothly between those of us on the Train and those governments outside that we still have dealings with."

There was a buzzing sound then, a droning that started at a higher pitch and got lower as it became louder. With a sudden screaming roar two more quads jumped over the far edge of the hill, they and their riders coming to a stop behind Andy.

"Son of a bitch," whispered one, pulling his goggles off. His eyes were tearing up. "It really is a lake."

His companion was grinning wildly. "And the Blue Train, too. Almost two miracles in one spot. Like maybe a whole new life is gonna start, right here."

The Blue looked panicked by this suggestion. He lifted his arms to wave off the thought, but then there were more distant engine sounds, coming from all directions. Andy turned in a circle, counted at least a dozen quads riding over distant hills on their way. "The network tells me at least three hundred patched into our announcement, Andy," said his quad. "Some of them are two or three days away, but they're all headed here."

Andy looked at the two newcomers; he didn't recognize either one, but there had always been too many prospectors. He reached down and picked up a couple of large rocks and dropped them into a saddlebag, then sat on the quad, smiling. "Well?" he said to the two of them. "What are we waiting for? Let's send out a few invitations."

The quad gunned its engine and jumped around the Jeep before the Blue could order his men to do anything, the other two following close behind. They raced down the hill, whooping and hollering. By the time they were at the bottom, water was coming through a small notch between two hills, spilling out and pooling underneath the wheels of the second Train car. A new stream beginning its life here, not letting anything get in its way.

Andy grabbed one of the rocks, flung it high and watched it bounce off a window of the first car. Faces started to appear, and some doors opened a crack. "A lake!" he screamed. The other two joined the chorus. "Water! Here for all of us!"

They splashed across the stream, and he hurled the second rock high, yelled more of the same. Now people were coming out, a few wearing Blue uniforms, but most just dressed as ordinary citizens. Some, judging by their age, who had maybe never been out of the Blue Train in their entire lives. At first they were silent as they stepped out, speechless at a sight many of them had only ever heard about. But then, almost as one, they were all yelling, some crying tears of joy, and right away more took over from Andy and the others, beseeching their fellow residents to come out.

Andy stopped the quad and watched as they splashed through the stream, mothers dipping infants into the flowing water, children kicking and splashing, one man in uniform even stripping off his coat and tie and rolling in it. More quads arrived, adding their steady buzz to the cacophony of joyful shouts and laughter, hundreds of people all out and together, under the burning sun, in one spot and sharing a purpose.

Andy gunned the quad, steered past a knot of old women who were crying and hugging each other, raced back up the hill to where the Blue stood by his Jeep. The driver and gunmen were no longer there. He looked down the hill, saw that some people were now making their way upstream, and finding the amazing source of the water.

"You can still lock me away," he said, "and get all those people back in the Train to go find some ponds that aren't too stagnant. But it will have to wait a little while." He patted the quad. "Keep broadcasting."

"Oh, I am," said the machine. "So are a few of the others, including two that still have working network cameras. We're causing quite the sensation."

"Good to know." Andy jumped from the quad and ran back down the hill, this time making sure he didn't lose his balance until he was right at the edge of the water. He knew before he got wet that nothing would ever feel this good again.

After this story was first published, the magazine's editor received a letter from a subscriber who had read it just before going to visit Hoover Dam with her husband. She apparently could not enjoy her visit, as she kept looking up to see if the thing was going to come down around her ears. This was a nice compliment, to hear that I'd so ruined someone's vacation.

THE ABBEY ENGINE

Stan signaled left and then swung the little Honda Vapor onto a side road that took them to a scenic overlook. Marty rolled down the hydrocar's window and let the cool air wash over him, the wind not so cold now that the car was going slower. The harsh sun made it hot inside, even for this time of year.

"We're doing well for time," said Stan. "Maybe five minutes to kill." He pulled into a parking space and shut off the engine. The older man opened his door and slowly climbed out, groaning. "I'm sure as hell not built for this sort of thing anymore," he said.

Marty grinned as he got out. Leaning against the roof of the car as he stretched out, he closed his eyes and tilted back his head, trying to work the kinks out of his neck. "I don't think age matters too much with something like this, Stan. Cram yourself in a tiny box on four wheels and then drive for eleven hours straight, it's gonna get you."

Walking to the front of the car, Stan looked around at the rest of the lot. Marty followed his gaze to the one other vehicle there, an old truck with a camper sitting on the opposite side, a couple about Stan's age bundled up in sweaters and sitting in lawn chairs on the pavement. "They look real to you?" asked Stan.

Marty squinted. "As real as they can be, I guess. Don't see too many trucks that age out on the roads anymore. Do you think they had it converted, or are they still running on gas?"

"Hope to hell it's converted," said Stan. "Although maybe they're just sitting there because they can't afford to drive it anywhere." He squatted down in front of the car and lifted a rock. Underneath there was a beat up rice paper envelope. He opened it and shook out two blue paper tickets, gave one to Marty and then pocketed both his and the envelope, all of this with his back to the truck and camper. "Had some people bag these tickets for me earlier," he said. "Easier for us if we don't have to show ID or deal with standing in line, in the unlikely event that anyone will be there today."

Marty tucked his in the front pocket of his jeans and then walked across the lot to get a better view of the lake. Not that he really felt it was such. Marty and many others always put quotation marks on the name; he'd grown up thinking of it as "Lake" Powell.

There were some houseboats and powerboats out already, floating around on the brilliant blue water, but most recreational abusers of the "lake" were either not yet here, still waiting for the high season to arrive, or else were sitting around occupying the southern shore near Antelope Point, borderline middle-class recreational types brave enough to float above a hyper-concentrated solution of uranium, arsenic, selenium and more toxics—to say nothing of vast quantities of petroleum and of human waste—but courage that existed only in the shadow of the new makeshift Southwest Militia base. If it had been night Marty knew that on the northern shore he'd be able to see the odd sputtering sodium or mercury vapor light powered by a secessionist's hydrogen generator, and probably the whole shore line glowing with the light of hundreds of small fires, desert rats and End Timers and Shasta evacuees and the like all smeared across hundreds of square miles of desert scrub like a strange sprawling city after some kind of reverse neutron bomb.

Stan came up and stood beside him. "You know, when I was a kid, the feds wanted to flood the Grand Canyon instead."

Marty looked at him in astonishment; he was still new at this, a recent convert to the true cause after years of skimming its surface, and constantly surprised at the weird anecdotes Stan was always coming up with. "No shit."

Stan shook his head and grinned. "None at all. Bastards wanted to build a dam and make themselves a big pretty lake. They even tried to justify it by suggesting that it would let the tourists float closer to the cliffs."

"Jesus. Who finally wised them up?"

"The Sierra Club. They did some ads in the big papers, suggesting that maybe we could flood the Sistine Chapel in order to get closer to the ceiling."

Marty barked a laugh. "Oh man, that's beautiful." He gazed back out at the water below. "Too bad they couldn't do anything about Glen Canyon as well."

"Yeah, well, life used to be made of all sorts of compromises." Stan looked at his watch, his face hard. "But not anymore. Let's go."

They were in the dam parking lot a few minutes later. Again, it wasn't too full, late January being the slow time of year. "Got your camera?" asked Stan.

Marty lifted his hand, showed Stan the new Nikon digital vid in the palm of his hand.

"Good. Make sure you record something after we get in the door. We're *touristas,* right?"

"Right."

"And remember that while we're in there I'm Mike and you're Jim."

Marty nodded, then looked back and to his right as they threaded their way between two other compact hydrocars. The span of the bridge that overlooked the dam reached across the river, rust intermingling with steel gleaming in the winter sun. A young couple with a Black Lab on a leash slowly walked across towards the town of Page. When they were about halfway they stopped and looked down at the dam, and then carried on. Even from this distance Marty could see as the man checked his watch, gusts of wind coming from upriver forcing him to hold his hair back out of his face.

Standing at the door of the facility were two militiamen, all camo and assault rifles and square jaws. One gave them the once-over as they approached, but otherwise did nothing. Marty could feel his chest tighten as they walked through the doors, but once they were in he was able to relax again.

The girl behind the counter was making an announcement over the loudspeaker just as they walked in, imploring those people going on the tour to meet at the relief map in the center of the room, and to make sure that they carried no bags, purses or camera cases with them. Marty and Stan walked over and joined up with the small group, only five of them including the tour guide, the others being a middle-aged couple wearing matching pale yellow jumpsuits with grass-stained knees, the latest sign of wealth in the Southwest.

Their tour guide's name was Eamonn, and he was almost the most irritating person Marty had ever heard speak, not only full of bullshit facts about how good the dam was and what a wonder "Lake" Powell was, but also with a tone of voice and a habit of talking that set his teeth on edge. Marty pretty quickly shut out his voice and just looked around, remembering every once in a while to lift the vid and capture a few seconds of footage.

After the introductory speech, Eamonn had them follow him to the elevator that would take them from the visitor's center down to the crest of the dam. Before boarding they were all checked by a security guard: first she scanned vid of their faces to check against files of known criminals and terrorists; next she opened each person's notePAD and made sure that it was a working model; then finally had Marty record something with his vid for a quick playback. Satisfied that everything behaved as it was supposed to, she pressed her thumb onto the security lock, then stepped back as their guide pressed the button to take them down.

The ride was a quick one, only one hundred and ten feet. They stepped out and down a hall that jogged left and then right and then through a glass door onto the top of the dam. To the left was the water, bathtub ring showing that it was down over one hundred feet from its normal water level, a mark Marty knew it hadn't hit in over a decade.

Above and to the right was the bridge, couple with the dog now slowly walking back from the Page side towards the middle. He walked over to the edge and looked down to the trickle that was the Colorado River, some six hundred feet below.

Here there were two militiamen standing by a missile placement, SAMS at the ready, nominally to guard against foreign-trained terrorists tried to slip in a missile or something equally deadly, but in reality there in case the Feds decided to try and blow up the dam and they were able to slip past the defenses being set up at the camp on Antelope Point. Western paranoia, thought Marty; the two other major dam decommissionings had proven to be monumentally unpopular for the government, and had prompted this quiet little rebellion in their own house.

The other couple didn't have too many questions, Stan had none, and Marty was intermittently recording images, so they hurried past the weaponry and along towards the middle of the dam and through more doors to another elevator. It was cool in there after being so surprisingly warm outside.

There was more aggravating patter from Eamonn as they boarded for the next ride, but luckily the elevator was quite fast, and they were out and in a hallway in just over a minute. Once they stepped off they turned left to follow Eamonn, but Stan interrupted his patter by rapping loudly on a skinny door that stood closed beside the elevator. "Where does this go?" he asked.

Eamonn tried to smile, although it wasn't hard for Marty to tell that he didn't like having his spiel brought to a halt. "There are ladders in the elevator shaft," he said, his voice flat. And then, almost as if someone had thrown a switch, he found his happy and irritating voice again. "Fifty-four stories worth of ladders. That's the other way out in case of emergency and the elevator doesn't work. Very tiring and *very* scary, I should think."

Marty was about to ask about what other way their guide was talking about, but Stan just smiled at him and walked on with the rest. He grabbed a couple seconds worth of vid of the hall and then hurried to catch up.

They walked for a good distance and then exited more glass doors, these ones leading out to a cement walkway overlooking a large grassy field. Marty tilted his head back and recorded the immense concrete structure hulking above them.

"Time to go live," said Stan loudly, interrupting whatever nonsense the tour guide was going on about just then. The tourista couple turned and looked at him in confusion, but Eamonn hardly stopped talking, just briefly glared and then continued talking about penstocks and access hatches.

But Marty pulled his notePAD from his pocket and flicked it on, activating the connection between it and the digital vid, and then piping any picture and sound from it to a live feed carried realtime to the web on a satellite that had been electronically hijacked for this very purpose. He wondered if the spiders they had sent out earlier were getting enough attention, although he was hopeful that as word got around about what they were trying to show, viewers would start to click in and stay to see what happened next. Stan had promised him it would be more than just a lecture, would be enough to keep people interested.

"As you may know," said Stan, speaking to the camera now and completely ignoring their guide and fellow *turistas,* "there are people who feel that the Glen Canyon Dam should not remain standing, that it should be decommissioned."

This got Eamonn's attention; he immediately pulled his own notePAD from his pocket and hit a button, speaking into it in urgent whispers. They would now have at most two and a half minutes before the goons in camo arrived.

"The Glen Canyon in Northern Arizona and Southern Utah was once a magnificent natural area, every bit as worthy of our devotion as the Grand Canyon, or Zion, or Yellowstone." Marty touched a key on the notePAD and it started feeding up info about the canyon; most people would probably drop it to a small line along the bottom of their screens, perhaps calling it back up later if this kept their attention long enough. "But in a sad moment in our history, the Sierra Club negotiated to give up the Glen Canyon to save another amazing natural area. Poor David

Brower, who at the time was leader of the Sierra Club and who was a hero for Mother Earth in every other way, died early in this century still feeling that he had done the wrong thing."

"How can you say that?" asked Eamonn. "The power and the water we've gotten from this dam have filled a huge void."

Stan smiled. "No arguments, Mr. Tour Guide. Time is short." He turned back to look at the camera. "As I was saying, this dam, besides being an incredible eyesore and wound on the human spirit, has already shown just how much trouble it is and will continue to be. Back in the 1980s a nasty design flaw helped it almost breach, and the hot soup of toxic metals and crap means that any water we use—for irrigation, for drinking, or for recreation—is deadly, more poison for us to add to the world around us. All of these are reasons to restore the grandeur to both the canyon and to the river.

"In his book *Desert Solitaire,* that famous curmudgeon and lover of the desert Ed Abbey figured someone could sneak in with a pack full of dynamite when they were getting ready to dedicate the dam, and hook it all in to the dam's wiring system, so that when they pushed the button to turn things on, it would instead blow everything to Kingdom Come. Reading that was the moment when many of us realized our true calling, our own way of saving the Earth." Stan leaned against the concrete of the dam, smiling. "When I was quite a bit younger, monkeywrenchers from Earth First! dropped a three hundred foot long piece of black plastic over the edge of the dam here, made to look like a giant crack in the concrete. Brilliant and hilarious.

"Eco-terrorists, you mean," said Eamonn. "Not monkeywrenchers."

"Spin doctor semantics," replied Stan. "Now please hush up so that I can finish." There were sirens high overhead now, police and militia vehicles rushing across the bridge to join in the fun. Marty ignored them, kept the vid looking at Stan. He still wasn't sure how this was supposed to turn out, seeing how Stan wasn't carrying anything that could do real damage, but any fine or jail time would be worth it for the publicity this gave the cause. This was a great coming-out party for his new eco warrior persona.

"It's time for a new paradigm," continued Stan. "Certain connections of ours have managed to lay their hands on something new, something that is guaranteed to change the Earth and shatter the very foundations of our lives. I carry in me the ultimate monkey-wrench, a way to flush this baby like the toilet it is." Stan closed his eyes, and then yelled, "Hayduke lives!" He grinned at Eamonn and the *turistas* and then at the camera. "More Ed Abbey, there; his great character from *The Monkeywrench Gang*. A little literary and ecological joke to launch us on this process."

Marty, who since he'd heard it all before had been tuning all of this out, now lifted his gaze from the screen. "*Did* you bring explosives?" He could hear footsteps now, echoing down the hall.

Stan shook his head. "Sorry to keep you out of the loop, *Jim*. I was about the only face that the feds and the coalition didn't know, and you were too new for anyone or anything to recognize you. Like I said, a new paradigm here. This is going out to the world, and I'm sure more and more people are tuning in to it with each passing second. They will be the first to learn that from this day forward, nothing will be the same." He grimaced in pain then, doubled over for a second before sliding to the ground. "Keep the vid going," he whispered.

Two militiamen came running through the doors then, assault rifles ready. But all they likely saw were a stunned tour guide and three *turistas* also looking a bit out of it, as well as one more who seemed to be sick. One knelt down to help Stan. "You all right?"

"What is it, Stan?" asked Marty, forgetting not to use real names. "What's doing this to you?"

"A nice parting gift, with me selected to be Santa Claus. Nanotechnology." Stan grunted, and sweat broke out on his forehead. He closed his eyes for a second, but then seemed to remember where he was, and looked back into the lens. "Finally worked through all the kinks, and by people on the side of angels. We've had folks, lots of them innocent and unaware, I'm sure, seeding the dam with nanobots for weeks now, making sure that there were enough hot spots for when the actual wrench was delivered. But the package they developed needed an preliminary hookup as well as a thrust from an intelligent source, and any computer I could carry that would be able to give the nanobots that sort of direction would require setup time and processing power that I wasn't able to carry."

He doubled over again, breathing hard. "As an added bonus, they use me as a kind of initial protein soup," he mumbled, forcing his head back up. Marty watched in growing horror as a tooth dropped from Stan's mouth and clinked on the walkway. "Break up everything inside, and then expand from there, taking instructions directly from my brain and following the orders I've laid out for them. Ow! Shit." He coughed violently now, blood and phlegm exploding from his mouth, spilling onto the pavement and over the pants and boots of the militiaman. "More painful than I thought."

The militiaman jumped back, swearing. He leveled his rifle at Stan's head, shouting, "Whatever the fuck it is, shut it off now!"

As if in answer, parts of the dam immediately behind Stan began to melt, a slow-motion waterfall of concrete. In its wake other pieces began to slough off, some dropping silently as they broke into dust, others crashing noisily to the ground. "Or what?" he mumbled, his mouth now almost completely toothless. "You'll shoot me? Please," a deep gasp, "do."

"Fucking right I will." He pulled the trigger and with an echoing burp from the rifle half of Stan's head exploded.

Sweet Christ, no! Marty leaned over and puked, heaved that morning's veggie omelet in a colorful spray all over the ground. In the background he thought he heard some more voices, but when he managed to stop and wipe the tears from his eyes, everyone else was gone. Stan's body was still lying there, but slowly disintegrating, like a stop motion vid of a dead animal in the forest being consumed by maggots and bacteria. And now more concrete was dropping off, some in large chunks and some just melting away, the area of destruction radiating slowly but steadily outward from where he stood. Already he could hear the ominous sounds of gurgling and splashing; he hoped to hell that it was only his stomach.

He took a frantic look up to the bridge. Sure enough, the couple with the dog was still there. He was pretty sure that they must have been put there to broadcast the restoration of the canyon from up high, give it the broader perspective. *Why the fuck did they get the easy job?*

Hell with it. Stan was dead, and there was someone else getting the final moments. He was going to try and make a run for it. He gingerly stepped over the bubbling, sticky mess that had been Stan and started running down the hall. For the roughly three hundred foot length the echoes of his footsteps were accompanied by bigger and more frightening sounds of destruction, of groaning from deep within the dam, the crash and thunder of falling concrete, and now the panicked yells of workers still in the dam, quickly coming up from behind him.

Marty got to the elevator first and pressed the button, but the light didn't come on. A few seconds later there came a great metallic shriek from behind the doors. "Son of a *bitch!*" he yelled, kicking the door in frustration.

The first worker to come behind saw immediately what was up and pulled a key ring from his pocket, fumbled with them for a few seconds, and then opened the door to access the ladders. He and four other men all pushed their way in ahead of Marty, yells of fear and anger bouncing all around him, all climbing as fast as they dared.

But already there was concrete falling and melting from inside the shaft, and it felt as hot as a blast furnace; whatever this shit was that Stan had brought, it was working its miracles mighty fast. Feeling now like he was going to piss himself, Marty reached for the ladder, but twenty feet above his head it broke free from the concrete and fell to the floor. He tried to pick it up, but the intense heat made it too hot to hold.

He leaned back against the wall, wondering what the hell he could do next. Something lightly tickled the back of his head, and he turned around to see what it was. In front of his face a large oval rapidly assembled itself on the wall, like a sort of slime mold with whirls of dark and light, two feet across and almost as high. It appeared to be glaring at him, like the eye of an immense and angry psychedelic cyclops.

And then, still trying to think about how he could prop up the ladder as well as dealing with this bizarre shape staring at him, a word appeared on the wall below the eye pattern, scrawled in foot-high letters etched into the concrete as if by a drunk using an especially corrosive acid:

NO

And then more:

SAYS STAN

And finally:

GO BACK

"Holy fuck," he muttered. As if to accent the freaky appearance of the words, there was a short scream from above, and then one of the dam workers fell with a sickening thud to the base of the elevator shaft.

Marty turned and ran out the door, banged his shoulder painfully against the far wall and then was running like a house on fire back down the hall, which was now almost as hot as the elevator shaft had been. When he got back outside he wiped sweat from his forehead and then looked up at the dam, watching with panic as new small leaks sprang forth every few seconds, hundreds of square yards of the concrete surface now melting like a nightmare straight out of Dali. How the hell was he supposed to get out of here?

He turned and looked around, then back down to the sidewalk. This time the same pattern was there, looking up at him, but instead of words, there was a ragged arrow beside it, pointing to the next set of doors. He ran. In the background, accompanying the frantic sound of his blood rushing through his head and his hoarse, terrified breathing, he could hear not only the deep bass sounds of the dam's suicide song, but also the high-pitched wail of sirens and alarms echoing madly this deep in the canyon.

The next set of doors led him back inside, to a small area adjacent to where the eight enormous turbines sat. All of them were spinning wildly, even the two that looked as if they were in the process of being dismantled for repairs. Their whining thrum overrode every other sound he'd been hearing up until then, even through the glass barrier that separated them from where he was standing. He looked around, hoping for a clue about what to do next, but could see nothing. He blindly pushed through the next doors, and then the ones after that, which led back outside to where the base of the dam huddled next to the river.

Here the sound that ruled was that of the Colorado, no longer a pitiful stream but once again a mighty river, throwing forth a deep and incredibly loud and primal roar that tightened his belly and sphincter. New rapids were forming, blasts of water coming from every direction now. Small inflatable boats that were tied up at the opposite side were bucking wildly; as he watched, one broke from its tether and was quickly swamped as it tried to ride the waves downstream.

The boats. Marty peered to the other side. *Now* he remembered what he'd heard but for some reason had ignored. There was an access tunnel blasted into the cliff face over there, two miles of it leading back up onto the mesa. He could see no vehicles sitting there, but with an insane amount of luck and some fast running perhaps he'd be able to get up high enough.

But there was a tall metal fence between, locked tight, probably to keep people like him safe from being fried by the transformers that sat in between. He looked over the edge, but there was no way in hell he'd be able to survive dropping into that maelstrom and trying to make it all the way over.

Another piece of concrete fell, this one off the ledge that overlooked the river. It rolled across the sidewalk and bumped up against his foot. Perfect size, but he was afraid to pick it up, not sure if any of this nanoshit would rub off on his hand. He bent down, hesitated, pulled back his arm, but then a high voltage wire snapped loose from one of the transformers and whipped through the air, the snap as audible as if it had cracked right beside his ear, barely missing the top of the fence and then smashing into the canyon wall, sending a shower of stone to the river below. Sparks scattered overhead for a moment, adding brief extra scattershot light as he finally grabbed the piece of concrete.

It took three solid hits at the lock to break it open. Marty swung back the gate and ran as fast as he could, still gripping the chunk of concrete in his right hand. He felt something in his left, looked down and saw that he was still carrying the vid in there. He thought about chucking it, but instead with two panicky fingers slipped on the wristband and tightened it. Stan had given it to him, and if he lived through this crap he could remember him every time he took vid of another bit of more peaceful monkeywrenching. Like maybe attacking elephant poachers with kindergarten scissors.

The gate on the other side was locked as well. This time it took almost a dozen swings to break it open, his breathing hard from the run and increasing panic making it almost impossible to get a fix on where he was aiming. But then it was open and he was running again, dropping the concrete to the ground and going as hard as he could, rubbing his hand on his shirt, trying to erase the invisible stain he feared was there to stay.

The tunnel roadway wasn't too steep, but rising panic and the little running he had already done had exhausted him. The best he could do was a kind of loping jog, staying in the middle so that he wouldn't accidentally bounce off a wall and fall to the road, or worse, plunge over the edge of one of the scattered openings cut along the cliff face.

In between brief moments of calm from behind Marty could hear his echoing breathing and footsteps, but mostly all he could hear was the death throes of the dam. It sounded now like larger pieces were falling off, although without stopping to look out an opening he couldn't be sure if that was maybe just the tunnel acting as a great bullhorn. A steady background roar grew to accompany these sounds now, the river below building to a fury it had likely never seen in its millions of years of life; there must have been at least a partial breach now, perhaps through a hole near the top where the dam was at its most narrow. Likely it was one hell of a spectacular waterfall.

He was almost at the fourth hole cut into the cliff. Staggering badly now from exhaustion, he stopped and leaned a hand against the rock, bending over and trying to catch his breath.

Heart not pounding quite so wildly, Marty looked out, squinting against the bright winter sun. "Oh, shit," he whispered. The river was already lapping up only a few feet below the ledge, waves splashing dangerously high as it boiled and jumped with rage. Upriver, not nearly as far away as he had hoped, the dam was breaking open in several places at once, a snapshot vision of water bursting forth in several huge waterfalls and taking more slabs of concrete with it, beating back against the base of the dam in a gigantic standing wave before finding its way on along the canyon. Unbidden, he pictured bodies and devastation. *Jesus, I hope people downstream can get away in time.*

He started running again, certain now that the water would catch him inside the tunnel and either drown him here or else wash him out through one of the holes to be swept along to death by freezing or drowning or just a good solid beating well before he got to the Grand Canyon. Maybe his body would pop up in a little side canyon some day, stuck in a tree, or perhaps his journey would take him all the way to the Hoover Dam, provided *it* would be able to stand against the coming onslaught of so much of the river at one time.

His feet were splashing through water now, a steady stream flowing uphill faster than he could run. Behind him, Marty could hear the echoes of the river as it fought its way up the tunnel as well as along its natural path outside. He was almost set to give up, to turn and face the water and let it take him, when he caught a glimpse of something red and white and glowing. Getting larger.

Lights! Someone had a car or truck and was backing it down the tunnel.

Marty started to run harder, but misstepped and felt the water carry his feet out from under him. He landed hard on his right shoulder and immediately felt the current trying to drag him both uphill as it rose and downhill as gravity made a near-futile gesture to bring it back. It spun him onto his stomach and in his shock at the near-freezing temperatures he inhaled, then raised his chin, sputtering and coughing, trying to chase it from his lungs. And to make things worse, the cold knifed through his brain like an ice pick, the worst freezie headache he'd ever felt.

He reached down with both hands to arrest his movement, only to have a wave come rushing up and knock him along again. Raising his head, he looked desperately around for something to grab hold of, spinning crazily as the water had its way with him. But he managed to find a ledge by one of the holes and grabbed hold just before another wave splashed up and tried to fling him over the side.

When he was finally able to raise his head for a breath and a look he could see that the car was closer now, but it looked to be foundering as well. Clutching desperately with his fingertips, Marty inched himself up the tunnel, trying to surf the waves that wanted to carry him up and then flattening himself against the wall to hang on when the river was trying to rush back down. It could have been almost fun if it wasn't so likely that he would drown, and if he could somehow keep his fingers from being shredded down to the bone.

It was another little hydrocar; seeing how close he was, the driver flung open the passenger door and yelled something incomprehensible. One last surf up also brought water splashing into the car, and so as soon as the drawback was over Marty flung himself across the open space, managing to catch hold of the handle. A fingernail peeled away when he grabbed, and the driver gunned the little car forward, Marty only barely hanging on, swinging wildly, his feet and the tires both leaving their own wakes as it fought for traction and hydroplaned like mad across the surface of the road.

About fifteen seconds later the road was dry again, and the driver stopped the car. Marty let go and rolled, this time scraping his chin and banging his elbow. He got up slowly, trying to ignore the dizziness. Swaying slightly, he started back for the car, then stumbled and fell back to the ground, face first.

A new roaring sound was coming now, starting with vibrations from the road and through his face, and then in his ears. He turned his head to look down the tunnel, saw the massive wall of water rushing towards them, and then a glimpse of the hydrocar trying to accelerate past him back uphill, obviously far too late.

Gritting his teeth to meet his end, Marty started to sit up but was pushed forward, something slamming into the back of his head and holding him down. In an instant everything went dark, and then for what seemed forever an intense pressure bore down on him, an avalanche of sound and weight and fury forcing him as flat as road kill. And yet he could still breathe, had for some reason not drowned or been carried away.

It seemed like forever, but eventually it ended. He was still in perfect darkness, unable to move at all, but the sounds and the pressure were no longer as extreme. And then, with a quick patterning of cracks of light in his perfect darkness, followed by a sudden return to normal, Marty was able to gradually sit back up.

Around him water was slowly draining away, taking with it the dust of whatever it was that had covered him. Downhill there was a new dam, a wall of stone thrown up and covering the entire tunnel, except for some tiny streams coming through cracks that only feebly crawled uphill before drifting back downhill, the immense rush of the river being diverted back down into the canyon.

Uphill, a cocoon of rock was melting away from covering the hydrocar. He started to get up, but felt a slight pulling sensation at his hand. He looked down, saw the same pattern and watched as new words etched into the stone, this time in letters much smaller:

SAFE NOW

Then, a puff of dust exploded from the road right into his face. Marty inhaled in shock, then sneezed, eyes all watery. Now there were more words scrawled on the surface:

SAYS STAN MORE TO DO CARRY ME/US

Oh fuck. Marty felt a different type of panic fighting its way out of him. *What the hell has he gotten me into?* He closed his eyes, wiping away the tears, then got up and staggered to the car, resisting the urge to scream in terror at what, against all logic, seemed to have infected him.

"Thanks," he muttered to the driver, grateful for the attempt to save his life even with the weirdness having suddenly twisted his life in a new and frightening direction. His throat was hoarse and parched, no matter the gallons of river water he must have swallowed.

Without looking he leaned his head back on the seat and closed his eyes.

"Glad to help," came a female voice. After a few seconds he opened his eyes and looked over, but before he saw her Marty knew it was the girl he'd seen on the bridge, with the guy and the dog and the vid. "What the hell was it that just happened there?" She was wide-eyed, looked terrified as she put the car in gear.

"Long story," said Marty. "And I'm not even sure that I know." He put his finger in his mouth for a moment, sucking at it where the nail had been torn off, not wanting to even think about it, much less talk. "Get good vid?" he asked.

"Yeah," she said, looking a bit disconcerted at the change in topic. She gestured down at his hand. "You?"

He looked down, saw that he still had the Nikon strapped to his wrist, after everything that had happened. "Yeah," he said, chuckling. "Good thing it's waterproof, hey?"

Even before my previous life as a professional photographer, but when I was deadly serious about taking pictures, Ansel Adams passed away. I sat down and wrote the most execrable and morose story I possibly could, and then over the next couple of years, as I learned more about the craft of writing, tossed it completely and started all over again. The result is my best-known story, one which brought the largest ever number of letters from irate amateur photographers to the photo magazine that reprinted it, and while I suspect if the magazine had bothered to tell its readers that the piece was fiction that might have calmed some fiery passions, I think the dent would have been minimal.

THE HISTORY OF PHOTOGRAPHY

1

There are many people who think that the camera is a relatively new device in mankind's long list of inventions. They're wrong. While photography itself is fairly new, the camera as a concept is an old and venerable idea.

Some nomads in the Middle East and Northern Africa probably understood the concept. Imagine sitting in a dark tent in the middle of a hot and sunny day, with a tiny hole in the fabric on one wall of the tent. The hole would act a bit like a lens, casting a faint inverted image on the inside of the opposite wall of their tent.

We in the west, however, have our caucasiocentric point of view. So to us the camera obscura was a revolution from around the time of the Renaissance.

The idea behind the device was understood in Europe as early as the year 1435, and by 1525 people were using it as an aid for portraiture. Paintings and drawings, of course, not yet photography.

For those who don't know what the camera obscura is, think of a basic automatic single lens reflex (SLR) camera. If you understand that without the prism the image would be upside down and backwards, then you already have a good grasp.

Now imagine, instead of a complex electronic machine all you have is a box. At one end of the box in the exact center of its face, rather than a lens you have a pinhole. Light that shines through the pinhole is turned upside down and backwards, shining an inverted image on the opposite end.

Take this simple box and add to it a knowledge of optics. A lens in place of the pinhole, and a piece of ground glass at the opposite end. Put a piece of tracing paper on the ground glass and begin to draw. A recipe for a near-flawless portrait or landscape.

There were other tools as well, but it was primarily the camera obscura that paved the way for photography.

1.4

The morning is cool, a slight breeze blowing through the trees, rustling leaves and waving small branches. Dew sits heavy on the grass, waiting for the first glint of the sun's rays to light up in crystalline brilliance.

I set down my pack, leaning it against a rock beside the stream that passes by. For a moment my exhausted breathing and the rush of blood in my head blocks out the sound of both the water and the breeze. But as I rest, sitting on the same rock, my own personal noises begin to fade and nature's take over.

I sit and listen, eyes closed, letting the sound form wave after wave that flow over me. I remember as a child, the first time that it struck me that Thornton W. Burgess was right, and that brooks really do babble. A delightful surprise, and one that continues to please me.

But eventually my time of meditation comes to an end. My watch has beeped; a half hour to get things set up.

First I undo the straps on the side of my pack, releasing my tripod. It's a Gitzo, 45 years old and far better than any of that fibercore or aluminum crap that is your only choice today. Sturdy but lightweight, when compacted it stands only a bit higher than my knees, but I can extend it to taller than I stand if the need is there. Not that I ever do.

The head of the tripod is not as old. Too many moving parts will wear out over time. Of course, there's nothing to compare with what I used to be able to buy, so I had a friend machine one for me. It has separate handles for all three planes of movement, and each one locks tighter than anything I've seen since I was just starting out. It cost a pretty penny, but I was able to cover it with money from the insurance when my wife passed away ten years ago.

The second I walked into this dimly-lit clearing a portion of my mind was at work, deciding what would be best to photograph. Now I have to spend a moment working it out in more detail.

There is a close-up shot I think I'll do, some leaves caught in a small whirlpool at the edge of the stream, but that can wait. Rather, I think I'll do the edge of the meadow as it leads into the forest, with the creek on the right. The sun will come up on my left.

I place the tripod in roughly the place I want it, then go back and unzip my pack. Inside is a smaller bag with some water and food, weather supplies and extra clothing, but only in case I get stuck up here.

I pull that bag out of the way and start sorting out my equipment. Camera, one film holder, two lenses, polarizing filters, light meter, dark cloth, focusing loupe, air release and change bag. Also a small tool kit that holds some jeweler's screwdrivers, a tape measure, duct tape, batteries for the meter, and a compass.

I take the camera out first. I attach the tripod plate to it and settle it onto the tripod, then open it up. It squeaks a bit, but that's only the bolts, and those I can replace. The rest of the camera is made of fine cherry wood, and I've kept it in the best shape possible.

The leather bellows extend easily, but those were replaced just five years ago. The last set were just about ready to rot away before I found a leather craftsman who was willing to make me a set to order. This was also expensive, but I don't have to use duct tape to cover the holes anymore.

Then I unwrap the lens and mount it on the front of the camera. I decide to use the 300mm, my oldest lens. I've had it for more than 50 years, and I bought it used. It's a Zeiss, aperture f4.5, and sharp as tacks from corner to corner.

The 300 will give me a slightly wide field of view. I can use it in this instance to get points of focus in both the foreground and the background.

The polarizer goes on the lens, as even this early in the day the sun will be too harsh. Then I get my loupe and dark cloth and proceed to set my angle and focus.

2

There is evidence that part of the photographic process had been discovered as early as 1816. In that year Nicephore Niépce wrote to his brother that he had used a box with a lens to capture an image in which "the background ... is black, and the objects white, that is, lighter than the background." This sounds a lot like what a negative would look like.

Unfortunately, he could not figure out a way to transform this into a positive image. The negative in all likelihood did not last all that long, and so what could have been the first photograph ever is lost in the mists of time.

Over the next few years, however, Niépce worked on perfecting his processes. He developed a system to reproduce engravings using photographic principles, and in 1827 took a picture entitled *View from his Window at Le Gras,* a muddied heliograph, as he called the process.

That may have also been the year he photographed *Set Table,* a much clearer image of some kitchen objects on a table. One lone print exists, the glass negative having mysteriously disappeared from the collection it had once belonged to.

1827 was also the year that Niépce visited with Louis Jacques Mandé Daguerre, a painter who had become interested in using photography through his use of the camera obscura in his paintings. The two became partners, but Niépce died four years into a ten year contract.

Over the next while Daguerre perfected his method. I remember as a child seeing a daguerrotype in my great-grandmother's house, a picture of her father when he was a child. The image was very obviously a photograph, but it was on a shiny old piece of metal.

It, along with almost every other of its type in the world, faded as our atmosphere was systematically fouled. A few museums still have some preserved in very controlled conditions.

2.8

Everything is in focus, the film holder is in the camera and the dark slide is out. I sit and wait for the sun to make its appearance.

There aren't many places left where you can see the sun as it rises. Its light is choked and sucked away by the black filth that inhabits the air we breathe.

Even here I'm not safe. By mid-afternoon I'll have to don my rebreather, filtering out the particles that drift up the valley as the day warms and as people in the sprawling city below increase their energy consumption.

But now the sun is almost up. I put skin cream on and pull my goggles over my eyes and move over to the camera.

Bulb release in hand, I watch and wait. When I think the light looks right, I quickly remove my goggles for a peek. Things look perfect.

The dew drops sparkle gloriously, and a mist is hovering as the water is burned off by the sun. The shutter clicks open for that ¼ second, and a moment in time is frozen.

4

I can only remember with frustration the time when I had more types of film to choose from then I could ever hope to use. Like most professionals not involved in wedding or portrait photography, I shot about 90% of my work on transparency, or slide, film.

When I still shot in multiple formats my photos were taken on any one of about ten different films, depending on the size and the speed I required. In 35mm I generally chose between four or five different films, in medium format three, and in large format I used two or three films.

As things changed in the field of photography my choice of films began to narrow. The incredible advances made in film technology were soon mirrored and then outstripped by leaps forward in other areas, mainly digital innovations.

Combined with all the problems in the world, I soon found my choices narrowed down to just one. Fuji stopped making any film whatsoever more than a decade ago, and Kodak only made 8X10 transparency film on special order starting about the same time. At great expense to myself, I might add.

So all of my shooting since then has been done with a type of Ektachrome on large format, which I guess I haven't really minded. For many years I had told myself I would concentrate on the big camera, and it took this to finally get me to mothball my Nikon and Hasselblad equipment.

Also, I've done my own developing for more than twenty years, as photo labs of any sort that survived the crash were outmoded soon afterwards. But that's okay; I feel in control, something I never did when turning my work over to someone else.

5.6

Although photography started out as an attempt to picture things more perfectly, over time people began to see that everything is relative. Each photograph is strictly an *interpretation* of the event that was witnessed by the photographer.

In photography, nothing is true. No, let me correct that statement; nothing *was* true. At the end of the twentieth century there were many types of film available, and each one responded to the influence of light in a different fashion.

The speed of the film, or how sensitive it was to light, was a major factor in how your pictures turned out. But beyond that, there were all sorts of factors. The same scene and the same light would render a dozen slightly different colors with a dozen different color films.

Black and white could be made to differ in contrast, even in the same film. And the latitude that most black and white films allowed gave photographers the freedom to do almost whatever they wanted with their pictures.

Maybe I'm being too technical here. Back in those days, I was in my late twenties, early thirties. The photographic community where I lived was, for the most part, quite static, but there were people who continued to push their photography forward, whether they considered it a craft or an art.

One photographer I knew shot almost exclusively with black and white infra-red film. Now, if she and I had gone out and taken pictures of the same subject, restricting ourselves to the same equipment and the same point of view, you would still have wildly different looks at the same subject.

But put someone with a different color film into our group, and he and I would still have images that differed. Mine, on a Fuji film, would appear slightly green, compared to his Kodachrome (or whatever), which would look slightly red.

But any image in and of itself would be a completely valid interpretation of the event as we saw it. Without comparing my picture to anything else, you would more than likely not be able to tell that it had any color shift at all.

Depending on what I wanted to say, I chose my film accordingly. I doubt that most people noticed, but many of my peers did. To me, that's all that mattered.

8

It wasn't long before the search for color began. Although most people didn't seem to mind the monochrome of the daguerrotype and other processes, the ever inquisitive minds of those at the forefront of photography realized that their efforts at recreating what they saw in the physical world were still incomplete.

Early attempts to capture the spectrum were fruitless, at least for the most part. In the early 1850s one gentleman in New York state claimed that he had managed to produce an image containing the true colors of its subject. Many people, including Samuel F.B. Morse, examined these photographs and confirmed that his claim was an honest one.

Unfortunately, the success could not be duplicated, and the profession went on with its black and white ways. The man who had created the images published a confused and rambling piece about the process some six years later, but it explained nothing of consequence.

Other attempts were made over the rest of the nineteenth century, some more successful than others. By the turn of the century, many different methods of achieving color had been made available. One method which attained a certain amount of popularity for some years was the autochrome, which Steichen and Stieglitz used in a gallery display at the turn of the century.

But in 1935 Kodachrome was introduced as a motion-picture film, and two years later as a 35mm still film. Then just after World War 2 color negative films were introduced.

Kodak had created a boom of amateurs when they had made photography simple some fifty years before. The boom exploded when color film became readily available for the masses.

11

Having replaced the dark slide, I pull the holder out and carry the tripod and camera over to near the creek. Halfway there I have to stop and put it down. I'm not as young as I once was, and my back and arms ache with the effort.

The picture can wait a few moments. I go and sit down beside the water, gazing at the bottom. After a few moments a small trout swims tentatively by. Even through the ripples I can see the cataracts that cloud its eyes, the cancerous lumps that form a crazy stairway down its back.

A water beetle swims by, and the fish lunges desperately as it senses the disturbance. The beetle almost escapes, but a quick thrash to the right and the trout has the beetle's backside in its mouth. A lot of energy expended for a small meal.

Anywhere in the world, the drama I just watched would have sold well on the nets. But I just can't convince myself that it would really be photography.

16

The list of great photographers is long. History would not be what it is if we didn't have photography. I could go into a litany of what photography has done for the world, but that doesn't feel right for me. I can state some of my personal favorites, though, and not risk the image of jingoism.

Ansel Adams. I had just embarked on my career when he died, a day that I cried; Dorothea Lange, whose sensitivity to the plights of those in the depression inspired many photographers when we suffered the crash of'07; Irving Penn, whose approach to commercial photography was so unique, so inspired, that he turned hucksterism into art; Alfred Stieglitz, who in spite of a tumultuous marriage to Georgia O'Keefe and allegations of pedophilia chronicled so much with a fresh eye, and was an inspiration and help to many others; Arnold Newman, who I thought to be the greatest portraitist of the twentieth century; Steve McCurry, whose work I first saw in *National Geographic*, work that figured heavily in my decision to become a photographer; and Dewitt Jones, who taught myself and many others the way to peace within ourselves and our photography.

There are many others, some of whom are even still alive. Compatriots that were a constant source of amazement for me, wringing freshness and originality out of the same tired old subjects.

Thank God. Without their inspiration, I doubt if I would have traveled this far in my life and my career.

22

The trout has gone on, feeling its way upstream. I get my camera and carry it the rest of the way and set it on the bank just above the pool.

First making sure that the tripod is well balanced, I tilt the head so that the camera is pointing down to the water. More than once in my life have I dived to catch a camera as it started to go overboard.

I can't risk putting a tripod leg in the water; it would upset the swirling of the leaves. But I want the shot to be perpendicular, not oblique.

Before making any adjustments I open the lens and look at the scene. The lens is too wide, so I take it off and take it over to my pack and wrap it in its cloth. Then I pull out the 480mm and take it back to the camera, mounting it and opening the shutter.

The lens is a Nikon, one of the last ones they made before a Chinese electronics company bought them out and canceled large-format production. It's not as fast as the 300, but I do think it's one of the sharpest lenses around.

Once I line up the camera, I adjust the planes. Perspective control is probably the primary reason people have used large format cameras over the years.

If you took a simple 35mm and took a shot of a tall building from the street in front, making sure that all of the building was in the shot, you would see that the building tapers towards the top. Called convergence, this is fine for drama, but not okay if the architect wants to show precisely what the building looks like.

So take a large format camera and set it up the same way. So far, everything looks the same on film. But the bellows in between the front where the lens is and the back where the film is allow a certain amount of movement.

With the camera pointed up at an angle, loosen the screws that control the movements and line up the front and back parallel with the building. Suddenly, you have a tall building that was shot with a built-in perspective control.

This is all based on simple physics. There are sacrifices to be made, for sure. If the movements are too radical, there will be cut-off where a part of the bellows gets in the way. And any tall trees in front will appear to be rather squat and round. But these quarrels I can live with.

Another use is something based on Scheimpflug's Rule; fixing the picture so that one flat plane is always in focus, no matter if it's right in front of the lens or several hundred meters away. That's what I'm doing now. The leaves in the pool are swirling around in a patchwork of beautiful colors, and all on one flat plane.

Unfortunately, because of where I am, I can not shoot straight down. So instead, I triangulate. The plane of the water surface I carry on in my imagination, and then make it so the front and rear standards of the camera are each on a plane that will bisect the first one in exactly the same place. When all three lines intersect, Scheimpflug's Rule takes effect. Everything in the photo is in focus, from the horizon to the camera.

But I've gotten too technical again. All of my life as a photographer, it has never ceased to amaze me to hear so many people talk of their technology as if that's the beauty of the process. They're wrong.

Rather, the beauty of the process is in its perfection. The fact that I can play tricks with the camera, using the laws of physics to further my own goals, that is magnificent. To use mathematics to help me determine my exposure, something no one does anymore, with all of their electronics; that is what is wonderful.

32

The aperture is a thing of mathematical beauty. Even though the numbers have been rounded up or down, the simplicity of the trail of figures, especially when combined with the speeds of the shutter and the film; these are things that made photography a craft as well as an art.

Start with the number 1, your maximum aperture, roughly the widest a lens can be open when an image is taken. Almost no lens has as wide an aperture and only rare technical lenses are faster, so for our purposes it will always be the widest, the "fastest" lens possible.

Now take that number and multiply by 1.4. Then take each answer and multiply again by the value 1.4. As I said, there is a bit of cheating, but that is for the sake of us simple-minded photographers.

1, 1.4, 2, 2.8, 4, 5.6, 8, 11, 16, 22, 32, 45, 64, and 90. A simple progression, from widest to narrowest. And as you narrow your aperture, another amazement from the natural world comes into play. Depth-of-field. The field of focus expands, and more in front and in behind your subject falls within your focus.

Combine this with the lengths of time that the shutter can stay open, and couple the ratio of those two with the speed of film you use, and you have the basic mechanics for taking a picture.

Or rather, had the basic mechanics. As with most things in life nowadays, a little knowledge is no longer a dangerous thing, because almost no one wants to bother with a little knowledge.

45

A moment under the dark cloth and the image is in focus. I then pull my old meter back out of my pocket and hold it down near the surface of the water. There is no direct light shining here, so the exposure will be a bit slower.

The reading is for one second at f45. I want to keep it at f45 to ensure maximum depth of field. In case my camera movements are not precise the increased depth will help keep everything in focus.

Ironically, the lengthy exposure will blur everything. The water and the leaves will combine to make a very painterly effect as they move while the shutter is open. But still, the field will be in focus and that's something that you would be able to tell if you compared it with a photo that was out of focus.

I attach the bulb release to the lens and close it, then insert the film holder in the back and remove the dark slide. After giving the camera a moment to keep still, I slowly squeeze the bulb and the shutter clicks open. In my mind, I quietly count "One Mississippi" and then it closes again.

The day suddenly seems very long and very bleak.

64

Shortly after I had taken an interest in photography, as a matter of fact almost coinciding with my advent as at least a part-time professional, photography began to take a much more electronic bent. Auto-exposure cameras were being introduced, and almost as soon as you bought one another company or even the same one you had bought from would announce an improvement on that.

Before long, you could buy a relatively inexpensive 35mm SLR that could make all exposure decisions for you. Point and shoot was the name of the game, and simplicity sold.

Changes in photography were like changes in computer technology. Unless you were very wealthy, you literally could not keep up. In fact, changes in computer technology were part of the reason for the speed of changes in photography.

With the advent of smaller and smaller microchips, SLR cameras were developed that were auto focus. At first this feature was very slow and unreliable, but in less than a decade after the first true auto focus 35mm SLR was introduced, photojournalists and other pros were using the top of the line models.

I worked at a newspaper for almost two years, just before the professional auto focus cameras were brought onto the market. At that time I was as gaga over toys and technology as the next guy.

But soon I saw something that disturbed me. For every photographer that was able to take these cameras and make something beautiful and feeling out of them, there were thousands who were losing their souls. The heart of what they were in the business for was being sucked out of them, and all they could talk about was faster shutter speeds, DX coding, follow focus and God knows what else.

So I sold a lot of my high tech equipment and bought my first 8X10 camera. Having to follow all the steps to get to the picture really showed me where I needed to be. It allowed time for self examination, and each and every one of my photos was thought about. No more mindless shooting because I could polish off five frames in a second, a whole roll of film in just over seven seconds.

Then, soon after I had made the switch, the major camera companies began to push the newest in photography; digital imaging. Although the first still-vid cameras were primitive and useful only if you wanted tiny prints, the world seemed ready to embrace them.

With the impetus the sales allowed, the camera companies improved their technologies to the point where digital photos were comparable to most 35mm films. You could simply erase what you didn't like, and the images you kept could easily be altered to suit any purpose. As with everything else in our society, ease became a watchword.

In the past decade I've watched as holography finally became moderately accessible to some, and that combined with 2D digital photography has created a boom unlike anything the field has ever seen before.

Need a great shot of your family? Just plug the Karsh chip into the camera and go stand with them. The camera will take a great portrait, just like Karsh always used to do (except in color. If you want black and white, just adjust the tone on your viewer).

Does your company need a picture of its latest product? Rent a studio and a special commercial camera and plug in the Satterwhite chip. Your very own commercial photographer without having to pay the fees.

Of course, it gets hard to buy real film in an atmosphere like this.

90

I finish putting away the gear and then sit on the rock again for a moment. I feel the letter in my breast pocket and pull it out, still not wanting to believe what it says:

> Dear Mr. Walker,
>
> It is my sad duty to inform you that Eastman Kodak-Davis will no longer be manufacturing photographic films of any type.
>
> There are two reasons for this decision. First, as you know, the market for film is no longer viable, and we were reduced to making films for you and a few others strictly on a special order basis. Additionally, the Euro-African embargo on precious metals has made it extremely difficult for us to purchase silver.

My apologies to you. I hope that you will see fit to continue to deal with us through our Electronic Imaging department.

Sincerely, SAMUEL FISHER,
MANAGER, EASTMAN KODAK-DAVIS IMAGING DIVISION.

I got the letter two days ago, faxed in just as I had come home from a shoot up in the Yukon. The air is still kind of clean up there, and there are even some animals still alive, if suffering.

I only had two sheets of film left, and that left me as a lucky one. I immediately tried phoning Simon, a photographer who had been on the trip with me. He had used up all of his film on the trip, counting on being able to get some more when he got back. There was no answer, so I immediately took the rail over to his place.

The door recognized me and let me in. After a brief search of the unit I found him. He was in the bathtub, dead, his wrists slit from hand to elbow.

I remember I wasn't surprised, just dazed and spaced out. I walked over to the house screen and thumbed it on. Sure enough, there was a note for me. Simon's face there, tears in his eyes.

"I'm sorry, Laird. You know why I've done this. First Jim, and now this. I love you, bud. Good-bye."

I shut the screen off and sat there, finally letting myself cry. Jim was Simon's only son. He'd died just four months earlier; the skin cancer took him. Simon's wife had passed on years ago, and I always suspected that Jim had been one of the main reasons that Simon had been able to hang on.

And then they took away his pictures.

I fold the letter and stick it back in my pocket. Then I lift the pack to the rock, and slide my arms through the straps. The walk back down is a long one, and the pack feels a lot heavier now.

Before I start down I look one more time in the stream. I can see nothing swimming in it, no fish, no beetle.

As I walk, I wish there were still birds to sing to me.

The only original story in the collection, this, for those readers not schooled in the world of post-colonial lit, is something of a re-casting of Nadine Gordimer's excellent July's People. *On reading that book I was struck by how it bordered on the SFnal without ever actually crossing over, and I realized that I could work with the idea. I suppose this is the closest I'll come to understanding how it feels to do a remix for, say, a hip-hop album. Which, as I sit here thinking about it, is ironic, based on my first statement.*

SUMMER'S HUMANS

They were scraping through the bush in the old transport: Jimmy and Kev in the back row of seats, irritably sniping at each other as small boys are wont to do; Jennie in the seat beside Laura, curled up and trying to sleep through each bone-and-kidney-jarring thud; and Summer in the front beside Cam, giving directions with waves of a slim, fluttery hand, brittle hairs falling from his body and littering the floor, forgetting every once in a while to speak in his halting English and reverting to the barking and coughing sounds that passed for the primary form of speech with his people. In the back sat three suitcases and five pillows, all they'd had time to pack before the fighting had descended on their neighborhood.

Laura was still angry with Cam. Three days ago, with no warning, no discussion, he'd come home with the used transport, a great, hulking monstrosity with six immense wheels, four long bench seats, and seemingly enough room in the back for their car, which he'd sold, showing her the cash in his briefcase and giving her that "don't worry your pretty little head about it" grin. "This is better for camping," he told her. "We don't need the car anymore."

"But why didn't you leave the money in the system?" she'd pressed, not understanding.

This time he gave her his "discussion over" look. It did nothing to soothe her anger, but at the time she hadn't been in the mood to go on.

Now, the trees and bushes on either side lost their narrow leaves as the transport brushed against them, blue-green pods every bit as brittle as the hairs on Summer's body. Their juices smeared against the windows and attracted hordes of tiny white insects, which in turn attracted larger insects and strange birds, all fluttering and thumping against the windows in the search for food.

Eventually they came out of the bush and joined up with a mud track that Summer insisted was a local road. The jolts Laura's kidneys and back suffered were every bit as severe as when they'd been driving through the bush, but she had no choice but to trust what Summer told them, even though his people were killing her people, back in the city.

After another hour they entered a large clearing, several dozen small mud and thatch huts huddled on the poor ground, smoke rising from holes in the roofs of almost all of them, and children—she'd never seen Mapaekie children before, but what else could they be?—running alongside the transport, coughing and barking and chittering, the last sound recognizable to her as a Mapaekie laugh. The boys sat up now, pressed noses to their windows and watched the native children; Jennie sat up and rubbed her eyes and began to cry, tired and frightened and unsure where she was. Cam made as if to scold her but saw the look on Laura's face, turned back to drive into the small copse of trees and bushes Summer pointed at. They parked there, Jennie finally done crying, now also looking out the windows, dread and anticipation both showing on her face. With a press of a button Cam opened all of their doors and the boys spilled out, chattering away to the Mapaekie youngsters, who chattered right back in their own language, neither understanding the other but all seeming to find a universal language of childhood, here on a planet many years from Earth.

Jennie hung back, pressed against Laura for comfort and familiarity, but after hours of her daughter sleeping on her Laura was irritated with this latest encroachment on what little space she had left, and shoved her away so that she could get the bags. This set Jennie to crying again, but instead of Cam it was Summer who was there, down on all four knees and crooning to her as he stroked her hair, leaving hundreds of his own short wirelike hairs on her head. She settled down for him, which angered Laura even more, and then Summer called over a shy-looking youngster holding a rough figure of clay, pointed to Jennie's chin and said some words. The Mapaekie child reached out and tentatively took her hand, and just like that they were off after the boys.

Laura felt the pit of her stomach drop, but before she could say anything Summer stood and looked her in the eye. She didn't know if she should feel fear or comfort; but Cam, all smiles, put a hand on her shoulder, and for the moment everything seemed fine. Summer grabbed two of the bags, Cam the other and his pillow, Laura the rest of the pillows, and they followed Summer towards a small hut at the periphery of the little village, adult Mapaekie stopping what they were doing and shielding their eyes against the sun as they watched the humans trudge past.

"You'll safe here," said Summer. He put down the cases and waved his arms in that funny way he had, extra elbows making his arms all waggly, and Laura turned around in a circle to take it all in: dirt floor; woven rug that had perhaps once been colorful; fire pit in the middle with a tripod of sticks standing over it; four cinder blocks, pilfered from the city no doubt, holding up boards to create two short shelves; and two clay pots and a battered steel bowl that she recognized as something she had tossed in the cycler back home two years ago. She turned to glare at Summer but he avoided her gaze, instead nodded and said, "Safe. Childs to play safe with our childs. My home," he tapped his chest and pointed out the open door, "is there, close." He stepped outside, still shedding madly, likely nervous as all hell, daring to bring them here. "I'll supper you tonight." He left.

Cam dropped his bag and set the pillow on top of it, then wiped the sweat from his eyes. "Christ, it's hot here. Shut the transport off and come out into the real world, enough to melt you."

Laura felt at the growing sweat stains under her pits and nodded. She'd been so caught up in everything she hadn't paid more than cursory attention to it, but it *was* hot here, hotter than she remembered the city ever being. "How do we sleep?" she finally asked.

Cam shrugged, looking around. "Didn't think to bring anything other than a few light sheets and these pillows, did we?"

"It wasn't like we were packing for a trip to the beach," Laura replied. She sounded bitchy, could tell by Cam's wince that he took it personally, but was too hot and tired to care right now.

"We'll pull the seats from the transport," he said. "They pop loose. Should be enough to keep us up and away from whatever the hell crawls around on the ground at night."

He grinned as she shuddered, then loped off to start fetching their new makeshift beds. Laura sat on the dirt floor with her back against the wall and put her hands over her eyes, choking back sobs.

Supper that night was a thin hot gruel that Summer delivered to them, five stained spoons in five wretched bowls, all on a scratched and pitted serving tray, everything recognizable to Laura as more junk she'd committed to the cycler months or more before. Again Summer wouldn't meet her gaze, and she was too exasperated to say anything. The food was bland and unexciting, but at least the flora- and faunatech that lived in their bodies would make sure they could survive off it. The children complained, wouldn't listen to Cam when he told them to stop, but Summer scampered over and crouched down in front of them, saying, "My food, childs, my food. Safe and good." He stroked Jennie's hair and briefly touched each boy's shoulder and they all calmed down.

Laura put her bowl down on the seat and stood, paced over to the door, biting her lower lip as she listened to him continue to soothe the children's tempers. She turned and he was standing beside her, looking up into her eyes. "You sleep," he said. "I'll be here in the morning." Then he was gone.

They finished eating, lucky if the children had more than a dozen bites each, picking hairs from the gruel and their mouths the entire time, then cleaned themselves as best they could. Cam took the boys out to pee in the bushes in the dark, all of them giggling, and Laura took Jennie to some other bushes and trees, carrying the one battery lamp, its light just serving to cast up shadows to scare them both. She had a frustrating few moments trying to teach Jennie how to plié so she could do it on her own and most of the pee wouldn't run down her legs, but finally gave up and just held her leaning back against her own legs, bending over with her hands under Jennie's warm armpits, listening to the sprinkle on the leaf-littered ground. Laura went next, and the two of them held hands walking back to the hut, Cam and the boys already there, Jimmy and Kev running noisy circles in one last burst of energy before bedtime.

The kids fell asleep quickly, though, exhausted after their first day away. Laura knelt in the dirt and stroked Kev's forehead for a few moments, calming down the nightly tics and groans that accompanied his drifting off to sleep, then stood and stretched her back. Cam was outside, and reached over to put his arm around her shoulders when she joined him. She felt the urge to shrink back but resisted it, and her husband showed no sign of detecting. Instead, she leaned in against his bare chest, arms folded against the fresh new chill of the night air.

"Sounds like the kids are settling in all right," he said. "Kev's even picked up a couple of Mapaekie words."

"They're pretty resilient," said Laura

"And you?".

She pulled away and looked up at him. There was no guile she could read in his face, standing here under the light of two half moons and an array of constellations that she still hadn't had time to really study. "I'm making do," she finally answered.

That seemed to be enough for him. He grinned down at her and then reached down and scratched his crotch, making that face he always did, like God had given him this pleasurable gift of being able to rearrange things down below. "We should get some sleep, too. I'm thinking we won't get far past sunup."

Laura nodded, stepped inside and peeled off her t-shirt and pants. She left her panties on, pulled a white tank top over her small breasts, gingerly climbed onto the makeshift bed and pulled the sheet up over her shoulders. Cam lay down beside her, and for a moment it seemed that the whole thing was going to collapse, but after some whispered cursing and frantic rearranging everything settled down.

"How long?" Laura had stared blankly into the darkness for some minutes before she was finally able to ask the question.

Cam grunted and she felt him shrug. "Dunno, really. There's a notepad in the bag, maybe in the morning we can have a listen, see if anyone is still broadcasting." By *anyone* he meant human, of course.

"Do you think our house is still there?"

"I'm sure it is." His voice sounded easily confident, and for a brief moment she felt the urge to scream at him, ask how he could be so sure. "There was fighting a few blocks away when we left, remember, but nothing was on fire or anything. I'm sure that the freedom fighters—"

"Terrorists," she muttered.

"The Mapaekie fighting for a new voice," continued Cam, "are not looking to destroy everything. I'm sure they appreciate all the advances that we've brought to their world, how we've raised their standard of living. Hell, I've got Summer's pay packet all ready for tomorrow. It's no wonder he's on our side."

Laura frowned, but didn't answer. Instead she let her eyes slide shut and fell asleep to the sounds of Cam's breathing and the calls of strange insects and animals outside in the alien night.

First light and Jennie was up, tugging on her mother to visit the bushes for her morning pee. Bleary-eyed, aching from sleeping on the uncompromising transport seat, Laura stumbled along with her daughter, knowing somewhere inside that she should be grateful a three-year-old was able to hold it and not wet her bed and pyjamas.

There was a low-lying mist in the village, mirror to a high blank layer of cloud that hid the sun. Already she could feel the heat rising, the humidity try to melt her away to form a puddle of evaporating grief and despair. Once finished they walked back and found the boys outside, giggling as they stood with their pyjama bottoms around their ankles, peeing in unison against the wall of the hut. One look from their mother cut off the laughter, though it was too late for the stream. Laura left Jennie outside, gaping at the lucky audacity of her older brothers, while she marched through the doorway.

Cam was just sitting up, rubbing his jaw. "I'm gonna grow a beard while we're here. What do you think?"

Laura put on the same shirt and pants as yesterday, every movement displaying fury, unable to say anything. Cam stared at her for a second, casting about for what he'd done wrong. The look in his eyes told her he was unable to find anything, so he reached for the next best thing. "Boys!"

Jimmy and Kev came running in, followed by Jennie, who toddled across the dirt in her bare feet and climbed up onto Cam's lap. There was a small wet spot on the front of Kev's pyjamas, and they both stood there, shuffling from foot to foot, looking down to the floor.

Cam looked to Laura, then back to his sons. "Apologize to your mother."

Both boys looked up to their mother from the corner of their eyes, heads still hung low. "Sorry, Mommy," said both.

Cam stood and settled Jennie lightly to the floor. "Good job. Now get dressed so we can have some breakfast." He strolled out of the hut and made a beeline for the bushes.

Laura caught up to him as he was just starting to pee. The hiss of the urine on the forest floor was louder than she'd expected, and she had to step back to avoid the splatter. Cam gave a momentary idiot grin which, after seeing the look on her face, changed to the scowl he thought showed concern. "What?"

"You had no idea why I was angry," she said.

"Something to do with the boys, right?" He shook his dick and slid it back in his shorts, but made no move to go back to the hut.

"No. Yes." She didn't ever fare well against Cam when they argued this early in the morning, but, as usual, she couldn't stop herself. "It doesn't matter. Just next time, ask, okay?"

She heard him answer Yes, but it was to her back. In the hut again, she helped Jennie get dressed, sharp movements prompting her daughter to whine. The boys had forgotten their scolding and were horsing around in their underwear, their pyjamas and clothes mixed together in the dirt and being trampled underfoot. But before Laura could say anything

Cam grabbed both Kev and Jimmy by their shoulders and marched them over to their beds, his voice low and menacing.

Breakfast was energy bars and water; nothing exciting, and again the children complained, but this time they finished everything. Before Laura could get them to wash up, though, several of the Mapaekie children appeared at the door, and with grunts and barks and squeals the lot of them were off and running into the trees. Laura hurried over to the door to yell to them to stay safe, but Summer was standing there, staring up at her, worrying at a fresh bald spot on his right shoulder.

"Childs safe," he said, repeating himself from yesterday. Laura stepped back and he entered the hut, looking her in the eyes the entire time. "You eat?"

"We did, Summer, thank you," said Cam.

Summer made some sounds in his own language, and three Mapaekie adults walked in through the doorway, one of them carrying a hairless infant in a leathery sling. "My wife," said Summer, pointing to the one with the child; the coughing sound he made must have been her name; it sounded a bit like "Cora." "My mother. My brother."

Cam and Laura nodded in greeting, unsure how they were meant to respond. All this time here, with Summer living in the shed in the back, three years of his being their live-in helper, and Laura realized with some shock that she had no idea how the Mapaekie greeted each other. Summer had come to them already trained, the agency assuring them he would fit in with little problem. When around Laura and Cam and the kids he had behaved as human as was possible. She did know how to interpret some of their different facial expressions, though, and could see that while Summer's mother and brother were at best diffident, his mate was not hiding her evident hostility.

Summer's wife barked and coughed and—here was a sound that Laura had not heard before—clicked her tongue on the roof of her mouth a number of times in rapid succession, the tone of each click rising and dropping and echoing around their little hut. Then she turned and walked out, followed by the others. Summer stood in the doorway for a second, pointed to the floor and said, "They live," and left as well.

"I suppose we'll never get a clearer picture of just how welcome we really are," said Cam. "We must have booted out the old lady or the brother."

Laura chuckled. "I'm sure Summer's told them about our house back in the city. He's been back to visit his family three times since he started working for us. As much as it's inconveniencing them, it's nothing compared to the step down *we've* taken." She dug through the suitcase for something fresh to wear, choosing to ignore the snort from Cam. "Hell, it's a step down for *Summer.* He's got this nice dry and comfy place in the shed behind the house, he's got his own chair and bed, we even let him have some of these blocks," she pointed at the cinder blocks in the makeshift shelving, "so that he could have places for his friends to sit when they visited. We're pretty much the only ones who even *let* their Mapaekie have visitors." New shirt and shorts on, she stepped out into the rising heat of the morning.

Cam followed after a moment, notepad in hand, thumbing the toggle to try and tune in any broadcasts. "Coverage is down. D'you think they took out the satellites?"

Laura looked up to the sky, exasperated. "Cam, these people were savages when we found them. How the hell would they be able to take out satellites that are up in orbit?"

"Dunno," he mumbled, still scanning. Finally the signal locked on a quiet, distant voice. Machine, it sounded like, programmed to give a laundry list of details about the uprising: aircraft no longer leaving the airport, the last two that tried taken down with SAMs; two shuttles managed to launch and boost into high orbit, carrying government officials to the abandoned station on *Hope,* the largest moon, but neither one had been heard from for over twelve hours; a signal had gone out to the nearest colony with a Regime navy ship, but that it could take four months until they even knew if it would come to help; about half the city was in Mapaekie hands, much of it in flames; the other three cities and sixteen smaller towns had not been heard from either; the regular militia had managed to regain control over the main armory and two secondary bases, and a counter attack was being planned.

"We can't stay here," said Laura. Cam was walking towards where the transport was hiding in the bushes, and didn't answer. She ran after her husband and fell into step beside him, arms folded across her chest. Halfway she finally prodded him. "Well?"

"What'll we do? We're good people, Laura. We've treated Summer better than most would have, we give money to all the right causes." He pointed at the sad little huts of the village, and at the Mapaekie out in the fields, apparently farming. "Summer and his people here have benefitted a little because you and I are so generous, but as humans we carry this collective guilt. We've beaten them into the ground, taken advantage of them, locked up and tortured their political leaders, and never really paid attention to how pissed off they were getting."

"All the more reason to leave."

Cam shook his head. They were at the transport now, and he was down on hands and knees, reaching underneath the chassis. "We're not killers, Laura. We ran, we didn't choose to stay and fight back. We have the kids to worry about, and I have you to worry about."

"You don't need to worry about me." Her voice was ice-cold.

This time he seemed to notice the tone, but instead of addressing it he just gave her a look and continued, grunting a little as he worked at something underneath. "Summer brought us here, and his people have accepted that fact. No one is going to rat on us. Hell, no one here even cares about what the city Mapaekie do, aside from sending home pay packets so they can buy goods or whatever from the nearest trading post." There was a click, and he grunted once more, this time a sound of satisfaction. "There." Cam shuffled backwards, then stood up, needle rifle cradled in his hands.

Eyes wide, Laura looked from rifle to her husband and back again. "Where did you get that?"

"Bought it, same day I bought the transport."

"I thought you said we weren't killers."

"I did. We're not." He looked puzzled for a second, then laughed. "Oh, I see what you're saying. No, this isn't for protection." He sighted along the barrel. "Summer once told me about his village, and he mentioned a watering hole where they sometimes hunt. This'll get us some fresh meat." He turned to look at her and tapped the side of his head with his index finger. "Thinking ahead."

He wandered off, somehow assuming the conversation was over, rifle hanging loose in his right hand. Laura watched him walk away, then sat on a rock next to the transport. Overhead there was nothing but blue and green, branches laid in place to make sure it was hidden from the air, as if the Mapaekie could figure out how to fly human craft, even if they had gotten lucky with the SAMs. Summer couldn't even drive, and he'd been with them all this time. No, this only guaranteed that humans wouldn't see the transport and wouldn't rescue them when the time came.

The windows and body were clean now, so no swarms of bugs and birds and animals were flitting about. She doubted Cam had done it, and sure enough, down on the ground, clumps of hair. Summer more likely than anyone in his family, or from his tribe. Still working, still making sure he collected his money, even in the middle of the greatest treason his people could ever commit. No doubt they were here strictly to protect his investment.

There was a cough and she looked up, startled to see Summer and his brother. It looked like the two of them were equally startled. Some words in his own language and the brother walked away, stood about twenty meters off, shuffling his feet in the dry dirt. Summer approached with his head down, but still looking up, silver eyes meeting her own brown ones.

They stared at each other for some time, the silence between them stretched out enough to make Laura uncomfortable. Summer kept his eyes on her the entire time, then finally said, "Go to see my bosses."

"Cam?" She felt a touch confused. "Why not just talk to me or Cam?"

Summer grunted, then shook his head as he had been taught to do. "No, no," he said, and reached into the fold of skin that, she had read, held his genitals and served extra duty as a pocket for carrying things. He pulled out the remote used to start the transport. "Bosses," he repeated. "Far. Other home."

"Where'd you get that?" Laura stood and made to take it away from Summer, but he stepped away and held his arm back, keeping it out of reach and making sure his body was in her way. Clumps of hair dropped to the ground. "Summer, you work for me and Cam. I don't know what you think you're doing, but this transport belongs to us, not to you."

"You live, I make sure. For me, now." He called to his brother, then pressed the button to start the vehicle.

Laura made one more stab at the remote, but Summer jumped back and she stood there, doubled over from the shock of this betrayal, hands on her knees, silently cursing him. "Yours like the other things?"

The brother walked gingerly behind her, opened the door and climbed in. Summer just made the barking sound that meant he didn't understand. Breathing heavily, she looked up at him, then waved a hand and said, "Fuck it. You know what I'm saying." Summer blinked his eyes in response, then climbed into the transport and backed it out, standing at the wheel since there were no seats. With one last look at Laura he drove off across the field, not seeming to mind about driving through the crops, and disappeared down the road in a haze of dust and stirred-up insects.

Summer didn't come back that day, and Laura spent most of her time fretting about the kids, and worse, about what Summer was doing with the transport. Were they already too much to bear, and was he going to hand them over to Mapaekie rebels? The children only made brief appearances, as did Cam, and when they went to bed that night the only talk was the boys, too wired up to settle down after a solid day of play.

The next day was more of the same, everyone eating a minimal breakfast and then running in their separate directions. At lunchtime Laura tried to call the kids, but they ignored her. Once Jennie stopped and waved at her, but offered no sign that she heard and immediately ran off to play again. Even from a distance Laura could see they were covered in mud; she shuddered at the thought of cleaning them.

Cam was also occupied, coming to the hut every hour or so and rummaging through their bags, then wandering off without saying a word. Laura told him that Summer had still not come back with the transport, but he just grunted and nodded, sounding for the world just like a Mapaekie. So she sat on the dirt outside the hut and ate another bar, watched the constricted world of Summer's village go by, and every once in a while tuned in with the notepad, listened to commentary on what was happening to her world, and once even briefly saw some pictures, although the reception was pretty poor. The images told the same story the earlier words had, though, and she wondered if they would ever be able to leave.

They'd had a chance once before, just after Jennie had been born. A Regime ship had come in-system, carrying with it a standing offer to accept a certain number of qualified emigrants for a new colony. Like most Regime worlds, the promised colony had no sentient indigenous life, and the people there made their way with more overt tech. Here, the promise of getting back to the land had fooled her people into believing that they used the Mapaekie for the betterment of both species, giving them *proper* work to do and keeping the humans from relying on machines. The fact that they had basically the same rights as the machines on those other worlds fazed very few, it seemed, and there were times it shamed Laura to consider herself a human, even allowing for how well she and Cam treated Summer. But the chance to move on had evaporated with a promotion for Cam; the Lands Ministry had need for people with his talent, and had made sure he would want to stay. She snorted, laughing in spite of her mood; his office had been one of the first to go up in flames.

Several members of the village walked by over the next hour or two, most of them studiously ignoring her, but two did stop and cough, squatting down with their strange legs and rubbing at their skin, creating new bald patches as clusters of wiry hair fell to the dirt, even as new hair grew in other patches. She tried to talk with the first one, but obviously the only Mapaekie from this village who had ever had contact with the outside world before this week was Summer, and so she knew better than to even try with the second, aside from a nod and a stare in the eyes, making sure that they knew she was not to be looked down upon, even as she sat on the ground outside a pathetic little hut in their seemingly nameless village.

Cam eventually reappeared, bellowing for Jimmy. Both boys came running, of course, answering their father after one call even though they had ignored her earlier repeated attempts. Curiously, Jennie did not come as well, a surprise, as she usually tagged along with her older brothers.

"I only called for Jimmy, son," said Cam, kneeling down to talk with Kev. He scratched furiously at his left shoulder at the same time, a gesture that both boys copied, immediately putting to Laura's mind that something had crawled up and onto their bodies during the night, or dropped from a tree or from a thatch roof during the day. She would have to go over their bodies with a close eye before the sun went down tonight. But before Kev could complain, Cam smiled and patted him on the other shoulder, said, "If you're careful and quiet you can come. Stay here for a second, though." He walked past Laura into the hut and came out with the rifle.

"Whoa!" Laura stood and put a hand on Cam's arm. "Where are you taking them with that?"

Cam smiled. "Told you. There's a watering hole not far from the village, and I've been watching a mother *caplik* and two young ones come for a big long drink. They came back again this morning, and judging by the tracks, they come by regularly." He hefted the rifle. "Gonna get us some protein."

This of course prompted the boys to hoot and holler in approval, even coughing and grunting, imitating the sounds their new friends made. Laura thought to argue, knew the boys were too young—they were only six and eight, for heaven's sake!—but knew also that anything she said to Cam right now would completely miss its mark. He was too focused, too certain of himself in this moment, carrying himself as the boss of all that he surveyed. So instead she just left, crossed the field to sit under the shade of the transport's hiding place and wait for Summer to come back. Cam said nothing to her, just herded the boys away and admonished them to stay quiet.

"Bosses to see you," was the first thing Summer said when he got out of the transport an hour or so later. His brother got out and stood beside him. Both had huge bald patches, tiny little hairs only growing back slowly for some reason; the bosses Summer referred to must have really put the fear into the two of them.

Laura put her hands on her hips, watched Summer flinch. It was the position she took when she was about to scold him, but all she said was, "When?"

"Soon," was his only reply. He pocketed the remote in his fold, and the two Mapaekie walked away, and Laura felt enough pride to not go begging after her servant—*former* servant—for more information.

After they were gone she looked about the vehicle, trying to find some way to ruin it, wires to pull or important holes to jam with clods of dirt, but there was nothing, no access that she could see. She doubted she could even break the windshield with a rock, and doubted even further that it would make a difference.

Instead, she sat back down and finally let herself cry, silent tears that tried several times to break out into noisy, heaving sobs, but while she knew it would help, she couldn't bring herself to allow the catharsis. After a few minutes she forced the tears to stop, wiped her eyes and her snotty, dirty upper lip with the heel of her hand, then stood and went to find Jennie.

It took an age to find her daughter, it seemed. When she finally did, Jennie was in another Mapaekie hut, sitting on the floor with the child that had befriended her—Laura wondered for the first time why she didn't know any Mapaekie by name except for Summer—the two of them playing a game that involved balancing a yellow seed pod of some sort on the tips of their fingers, passing it between hands and each other and all the while grunting in unison. Jennie sounded eerily like a Mapaekie; more than just simple imitation, she seemed to know what she was saying and hearing now. The rhythms of a child's game, Laura supposed, and she leaned against the wall and watched for a few moments, silent, torn between being happy that Jennie was coping and disturbed that she was coping so well.

From outside a Mapaekie spoke, *chuk-chuk,* and the two little ones stopped their game and turned to look. Jennie coughed, then stood and ran to stand in front of Laura, neck straining as she stared into her eyes, scratching at her shoulder and then the back of her neck. "What, Mommy?"

Not saying a word, Laura took Jennie's hand and stepped outside, allowed the Mapaekie adult who had spoken to walk past. It seemed to glare at her as it did so, but still reached out a hand to touch Jennie's hair on the way by, almost certainly an affectionate gesture. Laura responded by pulling Jennie further back, and with a glare of her own marched towards their hut, fingers tight around Jennie's tiny wrist. Instead of complaining her daughter shuffled her feet as fast as she could, struggling to keep up, hand dangling limply in opposition to her rod-stiff arm. Halfway there, her daughter finally asked, voice so little she could barely hear, "Are you mad at me, Mommy?"

Laura stopped, closed her eyes with her head tilted back and once again fought against the tears. If Jennie was crying and kicking and screaming, that she could handle. She let go of her daughter's wrist and knelt in the dirt, looked at Jennie's big brown eyes, remembered sitting in the rocker beside the crib when Jennie had been a baby, remembered promising her daughter that she would always be there to protect her, that she would be the best mother ever. And yet even Jennie, the daughter she had always wanted, seemed to feel more kinship for her dad and her brothers than she did for Laura.

The tears came, an immense flow that this time couldn't be stanched, and she was sobbing and her nose was running, everything cutting loose after being held back earlier. Through the haze in her eyes she watched Jennie hesitate for a second, unsure what to do with this strange sight, but then she leaned in and squeezed Laura, little arms wrapping hard around her neck, and her three-year-old daughter whispered words of comfort in her ear. She knelt for several minutes, ignoring the looks they received from passing Mapaekie, holding tight to her dear Jennie, until finally she could breathe normally again. She reached up and pulled the little arms off her neck, again wiped snot and tears from her face, then stood up with a groan and a slight smile. Jennie had been crying too, she saw, paths of moisture cutting muddy rivulets through the dirt on her cheeks. She wiped some away with her thumb, and Jennie cautiously smiled back.

"Let's just go see how your dad and brothers are doing, shall we?" Her voice was a whisper. Jennie nodded, and the two of them turned and walked back to the hut together.

Cam and the boys weren't back yet, so Laura sat on a flat rock near the door and had Jennie sit in her lap, then checked her over for any local bugs. Sure enough, a couple of them were nestled in her hair, and she crushed them between her fingers before casting them down to the ground. Clumps of hair also came out, although not enough to leave any bald spots like the Mapaekie; Laura worried over it for a moment, then decided to talk to Cam about finding enough fresh water to bathe the kids sometime soon.

The sun was nearing the horizon by the time Cam and the boys got back, and Laura and Jennie were still sitting there. Jennie had made a couple of half-hearted tries to get up, but her mother had kept her arms around her, belly tight against her back, so she had given up and just leaned back, head flopped to one side, seeming to stare at nothing in particular. Cam had the rifle dangling easily from one hand, the body of an adult *caplik* slung over his shoulder, blood from its wound caked and drying on his shirt. Each boy carried one of the baby animals, both dead with neat little holes in their skulls. All three of them wore smiles as broad as the sky.

"The mighty hunters have returned," she said. Jennie stood up and wrinkled her nose at the sight, but thankfully kept quiet.

"You shoulda seen it, Mom!" said Jimmy. "Dad programmed the needles to target their skulls, and he *still* needed three shots for the mother. She fought an' squealed an' just wouldn't drop!"

Laura stood and squeezed the flesh of the adult one. It felt tough, and there was more hair to deal with on such a large body. "We'll keep the babies for ourselves, offer the mother to Summer for his family. Fair?"

Cam raised an eyebrow, then handed her the rifle. "Fair. Hang onto this while I take it over, then. Kids, take your animals into the hut so your mom can start preparing them for tonight."

The meat was indeed nice and tender, although for a while she hadn't been sure if she would even get a chance to taste it. Even though they were young, the *capliks* had plenty of hair, and try as she might, she couldn't get rid of it all. After much cursing and fussing, coupled with the threat to just throw the damn things out into the dirt if Cam didn't come over and help her right away, Laura finally just decided to accept the fact that they would have a few hairs in their diet that night. She reasoned that, just as it would keep them alive and even give them benefits while eating the alien meat, the faunatech inside their bodies would be able to make use of the hairs that she didn't remove.

The flesh was seared, burnt a little too much in a few places, although still juicy, and it was easy to just cut small strips off and hand them to the kids when they asked for more. There were no vegetables to accompany the night's meal, but Laura had held back the second animal for a stew, and thought she might ask Summer to advise her on what would be her best options; if push came to shove, the floratech would even let them eat bark, but she wanted her family to retain at least a modicum of civilization and dignity.

After supper they took the children out to pee, and then splashed a little bit of water on their hands and faces. All three complained about going to bed so early, and all three were asleep moments after lying down.

Laura sat beside Cam outside, leaning into his shoulder until he lifted his arm and embraced her. They sat in silence for several minutes, just listening to the noises of the night, then Laura brought Cam's fingers to her mouth and slowly sucked on them, one after the other, tasting the juices of their dinner still lingering on his skin. Cam stirred and groaned, and she reached down with her left hand to feel his rising erection through his shorts.

"Mighty hunter indeed," she said, smiling up at him.

He grinned and took her face in his hands, kissed her hard, then helped her to her feet and stood as well. "Let's go inside." She nodded, already shrugging out of her shirt, his hands cupping her small breasts and stroking her erect nipples.

It was difficult at first, wrestling with the seat and slick with sweat from the heat, trying to keep from waking the kids, but finally Laura settled in on top of Cam and they found a rhythm not too dissimilar to the one they both knew so well, she leaning her hands down on his chest, back arched, slowly moving up and down, feeling the spark as he slid his thumb around the edge of her clitoris, his other hand massaging her breast. She came, sooner than she'd expected, gripped the hair on his chest and bit her lip, fighting to keep the sounds inside, which made it all the more momentous, and soon her whole body shuddered. Cam took his cue and with a distant grunt and couple of coughs allowed himself to come as well, warm fluids spurting inside of her.

She slid down and hugged him briefly, then stood with a slight groan; the muscles in her thighs would ache tomorrow. Still naked, she slipped on her shoes, grabbed a menstrual pad that she'd expected to use for her period several days ago and held it to her vagina as she half-jogged outside, squatted beside the nearest bush and peed one last time, feeling the semen cool in the night air as it ran down the inside of her leg. She wiped herself clean with the pad, then stood, rubbing her fingers together. There were hairs in her hands; she must have really grabbed at Cam when she came. She wiped them off and went back inside, meaning to ask if she'd hurt him, but already he was asleep. Typical.

Instead of lying down beside him she slipped on her panties and a shirt, then went back outside to stand under the night sky. It felt good to be in the cool air after the heat of the day, and she was still warm enough from the exertion of sex that she wouldn't be in danger of feeling cold for some time yet.

In the distance, a portion of the sky suddenly lit up. Laura squinted for a second, watched as it moved, listened closely. Slowly rising over the chorus of the night's animal and insect life, she could hear the pulsing thrum of a lifter, a small one by the sound of it. Someone out searching for them, at last!

She hesitated for only half a second, turning to look back to the hut, thinking about waking Cam. But he slept like a log after sex, and this might be their only chance. Ignoring her choice of fashion, she started running across the field as fast as she could, half concentrating on the approaching light, half on making sure she didn't twist her ankle on the uneven ground. She'd run about thirty meters when there was a cough from the trees, and out of the darkness ran Summer, placing himself in front of Laura, silver eyes staring her down.

"No," he said. "Not safe." She tried to push past him, but he held his ground, actually *pushing back*. "Stay."

"Are you out of your fucking mind?" she asked the Mapaekie. "Those are some of my people out there, looking for me and my family."

He shook his head; again, a strange sight, even after all his time in their employ. "Not people," he said, then grunted. "Not *your* people."

"They are *too* my people, you treasonous shit!" Laura was furious. She tried to get around again, and again he stepped in front of her. She grabbed at him but he stepped back, and she came away with hairs in both hands.

In the distance, the light and sound were both fading. Whoever it was, was leaving. And if they couldn't get the remote back from Summer, they'd be stuck here. Suddenly Laura felt deflated, lost and unsure about herself. She turned away from Summer, ready to go back to the hut, but two other Mapaekie stood there, blocking the way. Even in the dark she could see that both were losing hairs in large clumps, nerves getting to them like she'd never seen in Summer before.

She turned back to him. "What is this?"

Summer pointed at her. "Bosses see you now. Not later."

"What, now? In the middle of the night?"

Her former servant nodded.

"Christ, Summer, the kids need to sleep. They've had a long day."

"Not childs. Just you." Two hands clamped on each of her arms, and before she could think to start walking she was dragged off her feet, Summer walking ahead of them, scratching nervously at newly formed bald spots on his back and shoulders.

Laura struggled for a few seconds, tried to pull away, but they were too strong. She opened her mouth to scream for Cam but then one of them removed a hand from her arm and placed it over her mouth, and she was gagging on more wiry hairs. She kicked and struggled for several seconds more, then realized that they were not headed for the transport; rather, they were carrying her back towards the rest of the village.

They passed by Summer's hut, where his wife stood outside the door, watching without a sound as they hurried past. Laura strained for a moment to get a word out to her, any word, then collapsed back into the scratchy arms of her captors, not sure what she would even have said to the Mapaekie woman.

More huts now, each one with one or two Mapaekie adults standing outside, watching the progress of Laura and her rough escort. They threaded their way through the warren of dirty little buildings—were there really so many homes in this tiny village?—and eventually stopped in front of a slightly larger hut, long and thin and with a darker roof. In front blazed a fire, and three Mapaekie adults, two males and one female, sat on the ground in front of it, backs to the entrance of the hut. One male coughed and grunted, and the two holding Laura let go of her arms. Summer stepped in front of her and pointed to the ground; she sat, with the fire between her and the others.

"You would be Laura," said the other male.

She blinked in surprise. With just four words she could tell that this one's command of her language was far superior to Summer's. "You can speak English."

He held out a hand, smiled. "Of course."

"Summer and these others have brought me here against my will." She turned and glared at Summer with this, saw that hair was sloughing off his body like he was being attacked with an electric trimmer; he couldn't keep up with all the nervous scratching.

"Summer?" The Mapaekie male had an expression on his face that looked curiously human, like he was confused. Then he blinked three times rapidly. "Oh. You mean Horkit." He said the name rather than coughed or barked it, but even the sound of it in English was enough to throw Laura. All this time they'd called him Summer.

Laura closed her eyes and tried not to feel foolish. "Horkit. Yes." It sounded strange to her. She opened her eyes again, made her voice hard. "Why am I here?"

This time the Mapaekie talked in his own language, and was answered by both the male and female sitting beside him. The male went on at some length, double-elbowed arms swinging wildly about. When he was done the English-speaking Mapaekie answered, but Laura could see something was different. She concentrated for a moment, then with a sudden shock realized that this one had only one elbow per arm. She looked closer, and saw that he only had one knee on each leg as well. Was this a genetic freak?

The Mapaekie noticed her staring and smiled. "You've seen, but it's still not clear to you," he said. "We've been watching you and your family, and have noticed that the change is not taking place with you."

Laura leaned forward, felt the heat of the fire on her face. "Change?"

He nodded. "You are pregnant, I would guess."

Surprised, Laura's hand reached for her belly. She wanted to argue, but knew the supposition was right; she'd been ignoring her body since they'd arrived, but the signs all jumped out at her now.

He stood up. "Laura Van Ness, my name is Gahnok, but in a former life I was known as Rey Singh. I was a human, just like you."

"That's not possible." Laura shook her head angrily, then looked over at Summer—Horkit—but he was avoiding her gaze, staring straight into the fire as he worried at a fresh bald patch on his inner thigh.

"Think of what's inside you, Laura. Think of what was, and is, inside of me."

The realization came to her stomach first, such a wretched feeling she leaned over towards the fire, gut twisting, what was left of the evening's meal splashing sloppily onto the dirt as it forced its way from her stomach, unrealistically hoping the flora- and faunatech would be gone with it. When she was done she looked up, wiped away the blur of tears, and said, "I can't become one of you."

The Mapaekie who wasn't, Gahnok, looked at her and shook his head, mouth a grim line. "Laura, we have no explanation for why the techs in our bodies have effected these changes, but they have. Slowly, slowly, humans all around the planet are becoming one with our brothers and sisters of the Mapaekie. An interaction with some undiscovered aspect of the biosphere, almost certainly." He walked around the fire and stopped in front of her, hands behind his back, a human pose in an alien body. "My job in the middle of this Reclaiming has been to act as a liaison between the Mapaekie bosses and those humans who don't change, physically or mentally. People like you."

"My family," whispered Laura, brushing hair away from her eyes.

"The increase in hormones that results from pregnancy and breast-feeding keeps the changes from happening to human women." He shook his head. "Quite obviously, your husband and children are not pregnant."

The words shocked Laura back into action: she jumped up, staggered, didn't manage to catch herself before a hand landed on a log at the edge of the fire. She grunted with the sudden pain of the heat, pulled it back and held it to her chest, skin already blistering but nothing akin to the pain she could feel coming from inside. She turned and ran back towards the hut, and at the same time heard the sound of another lifter, somewhere past the woods, she thought, although the terror she felt was so palpable she could hear it, too, loud enough to make everything else a distant murmur, heart pounding and blood rushing, breaths heaving in and out in loud, agonized sobs. She looked back once, could see no one following her, and was surprised to notice that already the sky was getting lighter with the approaching day.

The lifter was getting closer. Out of breath now, Laura half loped, half ran, her good hand reaching up now and again to wipe away tears, desperately wanting Cam, the kids, her family, to come out and join her in their escape.

Close to the hut now, the sky lighter, and the tall, familiar figure of Cam stepped out, followed by Kev and Jimmy, and then Jennie. They stood and watched the sky, looking for the source of the sound. Laura opened her mouth to call to them, then saw Cam reach up and scratch at his chest, watched a large clump of hair drift to the ground, saw that they weren't her family. It was her hut, but it wasn't Cam, those weren't the kids. A Mapaekie male and three Mapaekie children stood in their stead.

She couldn't see the lifter, couldn't see anything other than a blur of color now, but it sounded like it was settling down into the clearing on the other side of the trees. Ignoring the calls coming from behind her, she plunged into the woods, desperate to be saved.

Printed in the United States
35528LVS00005B/79

9 780809 544899